"I'm just sorry about the circumstances that put us here," Warren said. "My family has used that helicopter company for several years and nothing has ever happened like this. I'm really sorry."

"Drake, quit apologizing." She walked over and stood directly in front of him. "It's okay."

He tried not to react to the look in her eyes, to that mixture of wonder, gratitude and…absolute trust? It made his heart flip-flop and caused stirrings below. In this moment, he realized the impossibility and danger of this situation: one very soft, very big bed; no luggage, meaning no night clothes; a romantic setting; and one of the most beautiful women he'd ever met. In that moment Warren knew that if this scenario didn't end with his making slow, sweet love to her…it was going to be a very long night.

He took a step. "May I kiss you again?"

She nodded.

It began with just their lips touching: soft, tender, reserved. But when Warren reached out and pulled her flush against him, and Charli gasped, the experience quickly turned hot.

Books by Zuri Day

Harlequin Kimani Romance

Diamond Dreams
Champagne Kisses
Platinum Promises
Solid Gold Seduction

ZURI DAY

snuck her first Harlequin romance at the age of twelve from her older sister's off-limits collection and was hooked from page one. Knights in shining armor and happily-ever-afters filled her teen years and spurred a lifelong love of reading. That she now creates these stories as a full-time, award-winning author is a dream come true! Splitting her time between the stunning Caribbean islands and Southern California, she's always busy writing her next novel, but Zuri makes time to connect with readers and meet with book clubs. Contact her via Facebook, www.facebook.com/haveazuriday, or at zuri@zuriday.com.

SOLID GOLD
Seduction

ZURI DAY

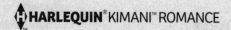

HARLEQUIN® KIMANI™ ROMANCE

There is such a thing as sudden wealth,
Often coming after one has worked to learn their self,
For those ride-or-die dreamers living life so bold,
At the end of the rainbow is a pot of gold!

Recycling programs
for this product may
not exist in your area.

ISBN-13: 978-0-373-86333-4

SOLID GOLD SEDUCTION

Copyright © 2013 by Zuri Day

HARLEQUIN®
™ www.Harlequin.com

Printed in U.S.A.

Dear Reader,

Just when I thought it couldn't get any better, I met the Drakes of Northern California! Like their vineyard-owning cousins, this successful family also hails from New Orleans. They've got specific ideas about how their lives will unfold, but as many of us know…life is what happens while we're busy making plans! Such is the case with Warren Drake.

Since January 24, 1848, when the first nugget was stumbled upon at Sutter's Mill in Coloma, California, optimistic wanderers have dreamed of finding their own pile of prosperity, their personal pot of gold. This resulted in the gold rush, when more than thirty-five thousand people from America and beyond converged on the northern tip of this western state and changed the way we looked at the land lying west of the Mississippi. Much like that nugget, finding love is also often unexpected. If we're lucky, however, this experience is life's most cherished discovery!

Zuri Day

I would like to thank all of my beautiful readers, who've embraced the Drakes of California and treated them like family. I appreciate you!!!

Chapter 1

"You're going to give up all this…and go country?"

"Yes." Warren Drake calmly palmed a paperweight, eyeing Richard Cunningham—his childhood friend—and wondered about the wisdom of his mother's request. Even more, he was second-guessing the sanity of his agreeing to do what she wanted.

The fact was, in leaving his plush condo located in the tony town of Paradise Cove and "going country," as Richard put it, Warren wasn't giving up anything. By moving twenty miles east of where he'd grown up to the sprawling countryside, he was gaining a front-row view to the business he'd cultivated for the past five years—almost seven hundred acres of top-quality grapes. This was one of the most lucrative crops one could grow in California, and taking his cousin Donovan Drake's advice to do so was one of the best business decisions he'd ever made. But Richard didn't need to know this. Because of his mother's kindness, this New Orleans native whom Warren had known since childhood was deep enough in the Drake pockets already.

"If you're having second thoughts about working with me and thinking about going back south, I understand." *And I'd be grateful.*

"No, man, your mother was kind enough to give me a chance, helping me to get back on my feet after all this time spent away, to get a new start in life. I'm going to try and do her proud, War. And honor the memory of my mom."

Warren nodded. Maybe he was being too hard on Richard, too judgmental. Unlike Warren, who'd grown up in a comfortable, loving two-parent family, Richard had grown up in a single-parent family, on the bad side of town, barely knowing his father and basically being the man of the house by the time he was ten. He'd met Warren's grandfather Walter during a mentor program sponsored by the Boys & Girls Club and became a fixture in the elder man's household. During Warren's summers spent in New Orleans and frequent visits in between, the two became as close as brothers. They'd even chosen to attend the same college and roomed together for a time. Then came senior year and Richard's bad choices. Errant focus. Wrong crowd. He dropped out of college and began dabbling in illegal activities. Warren flourished in the family business. Richard floundered in jail. They hadn't seen each other in eight or nine years.

"So are you sure you can handle it, Rich? Working construction? I don't remember you ever working with your hands."

"I'm a quick learner. But I still think you should make me a supervisor. I'm a born leader, man. And I'm used to managing a crew. The product I was pushing may have been illegal, but while it lasted my ship was tight!"

Warren shook his head as he answered his ringing phone. "Hey, Jackson. What's up?" He paused to listen, and watched as Richard picked up and examined the paperweight. "All right, then. I'll see you in about fifteen." He ended the call and stood. "That was my brother-in-law. He's at the site. You want to roll out with me?"

"Sure." Richard palmed the paperweight. "Is this solid gold, man?"

"Yes. Mined right in this part of the country."

"Word?"

Warren said nothing further, and silently berated himself for that slip of the tongue. He'd known Richard his whole life, but they were no longer close. People changed. He reminded himself that the less this former best friend knew about what had once been found on his family's land—and anything else about the family businesses— the better.

Picture-perfect scenery flew by them as Warren's sporty Maserati ate up the short distance between his condo located in the gated community of Golden Gates and the property located in what would one day be zoned as Paradise Valley. The weather had turned hot on this August afternoon, lazy clouds floated across an azure-blue sky and sunflowers dotted the landscape before row after row of grapevines, encased by a newly built wrought-iron fence, signaled the beginning of Drake land. He turned onto a plot that had been cleared for building, noting Jackson's rented pickup and another car belonging to the local subcontractor. The two men exited the car, careful of the jutting rocks and clods of soil.

"Mr. Wright!"

"Mr. Drake!"

They gave each other a fist pound.

"Boss, this is an old friend of mine, Richard Cunningham. Richard, this is my brother-in-law, Jackson 'Boss' Wright, owner of one of the best construction companies this side of the Mississippi."

Richard stepped forward, hand outstretched. "Boss, huh? A pleasure."

Jackson shook it. "Yes, but I had the nickname before owning a company. My mother gave it to me when I was about two years old and owned nothing, not even the wet diaper on my behind."

The men laughed. Warren nodded at the roll of paper that Jackson was holding. "So what have we here?"

"The final blueprints for your house." He pointed to various sticks with twine around them. "We've got everything marked out, rooms, deck, swimming pool, guest houses and the expansion for your stables. Just wanted to walk you through everything one final time before we get started. If everything meets your approval, we'll start excavating for the foundation right away. Brandon, the foreman, will keep things flowing smoothly during the days that I'm gone."

"I'm ready to get started," Warren said, rubbing his hands in excitement. "Let's..." The sentence died on his tongue as the sound of hard-hitting hoofbeats caught his ear. As one, the three men turned toward the sound. A lone rider, looking strong and sure in the saddle, was approaching. He wore jeans, an oversize button-down shirt, a cowboy hat and a red bandanna over his mouth and nose. The rider jumped a small bush in the horse's path effortlessly, standing in the stirrups as the horse landed, then continued to what was his clear destination—them.

"Good rider," Warren mumbled, clearly impressed.

"A real-life cowboy," Richard drawled. "You're going country for real."

The rider reached them and pulled up on the reins. From his superior position, he peered in silence, eyes shielded with a pair of dark shades. After a few seconds he dismounted, pulled down the kerchief and took off his hat.

The three men stepped back in unison, brows raised, dumbstruck.

Long curly hair tumbled around the rider's shoulders and lips that at least one man guessed were soft and quite attractive were fixed in a firm line. A slender hand pushed the dark glasses up on her head and the hair from her face. Chocolate orbs framed by curly black lashes seared them with their intensity.

A subtle look of incredulity passed between the men.

He was a *she?*

Indeed. And a sexy she at that.

But Ms. Sexy did not look happy.

"Charli Reed," she announced, her eyes narrowed, her stance defensive. "Is one of you the owner of this place?"

Warren stepped forward. "I am. Warren Drake." He held out his hand, noting a flash of something—*recognition, maybe*—in her eyes. "Are you my neighbor?"

"I am," she replied, ignoring his outstretched hand and crossing her arms instead. "And we've got a problem."

Chapter 2

"**Y**ou've got a problem?" Richard, pretty boy and eternal ladies' man, took a step toward Charli, eyeing her much like a hungry dog would a biscuit. "Well, baby girl…I'm a problem solver."

If looks could kill, for Richard it would have been time for ashes to ashes and dust to dust. Her eyes slid from him to Jackson and back before returning to Warren.

Richard backed up, holding up his hands in mock surrender.

"I've got a problem with your fence. You've enclosed the stream that my cows have used for the last ten years. The next water source is two miles away."

Warren's first thought was wondering how her cows were his problem. He didn't have long to wait for clarification.

"That stream is on Reed land."

Warren looked at Jackson, who gave a slight nod and walked to a large black pickup. "My people had the land surveyed five years ago, when the first vines were planted. The fence was erected based on those specs."

"I don't care what the paper says. That stream is for my cows. We need access. You need to move your fence."

Warren scowled. Who did this gorgeous cup of cocoa think she was? "I'm sorry, but you must be mistaken."

Jackson returned from his truck with survey in hand. He unrolled it, giving one end to Warren to hold while he held the other and pointed to property lines. "Here is the lake, Ms. Reed," he said, pointing to the paper. "And here is the Drake property line."

Charli glanced at the paper and said nothing.

"We had everything double-checked before we erected the fence," Warren said as Jackson rolled up the proof and placed it under his arm. "Not only against the original paperwork filed at the courthouse, but with another top-rate surveyor." He crossed his arms, matching her stance. "All of the property within the fence is mine."

"How many acres is this—" she spread her arms "—property of yours?"

"I can't see how that's any of your business."

"Maybe not. But it's a shame that with all that you own we're standing here squabbling about a half acre or less that you probably won't even see, let alone that you'll need."

"Be that as it may, it's my land and my fence."

A stare-off ensued, during which time Warren took note of a few things: the color of her eyes, her kissable long neck and how even with an oversize shirt he could tell that she was wearing the hell out of that pair of jeans.

"My contractor and I need to get back to work. Is there anything else I can do for you?"

"Yes." Charli spun on her heel, placed a well-worn boot into the stirrup and swung up onto the chestnut-colored stallion in one fluid motion. "You can go to hell."

Warren watched the trail of dust that followed his feisty neighbor down the winding drive. "You know," he drawled to Jackson and Richard as she rounded the bend and galloped out of sight. "I think Miss Charli needs to learn how to say how she really feels."

Charli used long, strong brushstrokes on the horse's coat, thankful to have something to do. She was still ticked off—okay, livid—after her encounter with her jerk of a neighbor, Warren Drake. Even after riding hard all the way home, going past her house and giving the horse his head for a good five minutes. After helping the ranch hands round up a herd of cattle, and tossing up heavy bales of hay for the next day's feeding, there was still enough pent-up frustration for her to go fifteen rounds with a punching bag. Or a neighbor.

For the past two years, ever since she'd returned to the land she loved and regained the reins of her grandfather Charles Reed's dream to stave off a foreclosure, Charli had been exhausted but content. She'd finally found the peace that had eluded her for the past few years, peace that had first been shattered when her grandfather—her rock—died, and then had further been obliterated by the dissolution of an engagement that never should have occurred. Coming back to the ranch had been like coming home. Most of the old hands still worked there, and treated her with the respect they'd given Charles Reed. The house manager, whom she called her play uncle, Griff, was now the closest thing she had to family and treated her like his own. It hadn't hurt that all of them had known her since she was knee-high to a gnat, or that she could ride and rope with the best of them—a country girl through and through.

"I can't believe the audacity of that man," she grumbled in time with the brushstroke. *Or how tall and handsome he is, or how his muscles flexed when he crossed his arms.*

"Arrogant jerk." *Blessed with a cleft* and *dimples? How unfair!* Her grandfather had talked about the Drakes, how they'd swept into town decades ago, buying up acres of land. What had once been miles and miles of empty fields eventually became Paradise Cove, incorporated by Walter's son, Ike Drake Sr., and his highbrow friends.

"They're a bunch of self-absorbed, bourgie possums, Gramps, just like you said." But what he hadn't told her was how handsome a Drake man could be, or what to do when just five minutes in his presence had made her heart go boom.

Chapter 3

"Son! This is a surprise." Jennifer Drake stood back from the door so that Warren could enter the oversize foyer.

"Hello, Mom."

She reached up to give him a hug. "Where are Richard and Jackson?"

"Dropped Richard back off at his apartment. As we were wrapping up, Boss got a phone call that forced him to cancel his plans to join us."

"From whom?"

"Diamond. She flew up to surprise him with a romantic weekend in San Francisco."

"Oh, that's a lovely thing for his wife to do."

Warren's father, Ike, came around the corner, a predinner tumbler of scotch in hand. "Hey there, Warren. How'd it go today?"

"It was interesting."

"Son, can I fix you a drink?"

"Sure, Mom. Thanks."

"Will you be staying for dinner? The twins are coming over."

"Don't they always?" They could consume a whole pig between the two of them, but it was no secret that neither Terrell nor Teresa, Warren's younger siblings by two years, liked to cook. "What about Niko?"

"Out on a date." Jennifer didn't try and hide her chagrin for Warren's older brother's choice.

"He must be with Ashley."

"I don't know why he can't see what's painfully obvious. That girl is chasing dollar signs."

"Now, Jennifer," Ike said, his voice somber and a tad chiding. "He's a grown man. We've done our job in raising him. He has to make his own way."

Jennifer prepared to say something, thought better of it and left the room to get Warren's scotch.

"Come on, son." Ike headed into the great room. Warren followed behind, noting the vases of colorful and fresh flowers they passed on the way, evidence of his mother's artistic hand. When he married, Warren wanted someone like her: beautiful, strong, intelligent, classy.

His father took a seat in one of two leather wingback chairs. Warren took the other one. "So you say your day was interesting. How so?"

"I met my neighbor." Ike took a sip as he nodded, listened. "She wasn't too happy to see me."

"She?"

"That was my reaction." He paused as Jennifer brought in his tumbler of scotch. He took a taste as his mother sat on the nearby couch. "Her name is Charli Reed."

"Reed?" his parents said at once.

He looked from one to the other and didn't miss their raised-brow exchange. "What's up with that reaction?"

"Just surprised, son, that's all. We thought the Reeds had sold that place a few years ago, after Charles died."

"Who's Charles?"

"He used to be in business with your grandfather," Jennifer offered, placing her crystal flute of sherry on the table.

"It was after he was honorably discharged from the service."

"After his injury?"

Ike nodded. "They had another buddy who told him about the property, which at that time went for pennies on the dollar. They bought up all one thousand acres and at one time had a modestly profitable dairy farm."

"Then on a trip back home to New Orleans he met your grandmother and moved back home." Jennifer sat back on the couch and wiped a nonexistent wrinkle from her slacks. "But you've heard this story, Warren. I've heard Grandpa sharing it with you boys."

"I guess I wasn't paying attention."

"What happened when you met the woman?" Ike asked.

"She came galloping up on this impressive-looking horse, dismounted and demanded I move my fence. Said her cattle needed access to the stream on our land."

"Ike, do you think that's his granddaughter?"

He nodded at Jennifer. "Sounds like it. You said her name is Charli?"

"Yes," Warren replied.

"Then that's her."

"So our grandfathers owned a business together once. That still doesn't explain her nasty attitude."

Ike leaned back, stretched his long legs out in front of him. "Their parting, which started out amicably, soured over the years."

"What happened?" Both parents were slow to respond. "Wait, this doesn't have anything to do with the gold, does it?"

"Not really," Jennifer said. "They found what little bit

of gold there was when the property was owned jointly and split it fifty-fifty."

"So what was it then?"

"When Daddy decided to move back to New Orleans, the dairy was doing fairly well but the cash flow wasn't exceptional. He helped Charles by buying up the acres that weren't being used—"

"Six hundred acres, right?" That's how many acres there had been before Warren had purchased several hundred more.

"Seven hundred initially," Ike continued. "Daddy bought the land, Charles kept the business. They shook hands and all was well."

Jennifer continued the story. "Several years later, Charles came to your grandfather and asked to buy back some land. Daddy Walter wasn't keen on it but Charles was persistent, saying that he needed more land for the cows. Finally, Daddy Walter agreed to sell him one hundred acres—at a price well below market value I might add—but that was it. Later, when the dairy farm experienced an exceptionally good year financially, he asked to buy back more of the land. Charles knew how well your grandfather had done in real estate and didn't see why he was interested in holding on to property he didn't even visit. He asked more than once. Each time Daddy Walter refused, finally letting him know in no uncertain terms that what he'd purchased would remain Drake property. Their relationship was never the same after that."

"Daddy thought that Charles might have heard rumors about more gold on the land and was resentful over that, though Charles denied it," Ike said.

"Could that be possible? Is there more gold on the land?"

"I don't think so, Warren. We all know the history and Daddy and Charles had surely heard the rumors. They spent a good deal of time and money searching when they first moved here, but aside from that one small vein that was found and mined, they had no luck. I think if there was any grand buried treasure, they would have found it."

The doorbell rang, followed by the sounds of several people entering the house.

"That would be your brother and sister," Jennifer said. "In here, children!" She left the room to greet them.

"So do you think I should move the fence, Dad?"

"That's going to have to be your call, son. But just remember, if you give some people an inch…they'll take a mile."

Warren and Ike joined Jennifer and his siblings at the table. Talk of land and fences was replaced with that of plans for the town's annual Days of Paradise Gala, a three-day event celebrating the town's beginning. Fairgrounds would be set up on the north end of town. There would be a parade, various contests and the pinnacle of the festivities: the Paradise Ball. The women conversed about what family favorite Jennifer should bake for the pie contest, and what designer original they'd wear to the dance. The men talked about how Drake Realty Plus would be showcased in the parade. Niko had secured a fully restored 1975 Caprice convertible—metallic gold with wide, white rims. The car, built in the year that Paradise Cove had been incorporated, would tow a thirty-foot billboard specially designed for the day, covered with a mural of old and modern-day Paradise Cove and containing the words *Drake Realty: Homes with a Heart for 30 Years…and Counting!* Throughout the appetizer, entrée and dessert they talked, laughed and strategized. Warren answered questions when asked and commented as needed. But his mind wasn't on the upcoming festivities. It was on a feisty woman with an attitude and a body that made his blood boil.

Give some people an inch…they'll take a mile. That's

what his father had said. *Well, Daddy,* Warren thought as he watched his mother pour cups of tea. *I might just have to take that chance.*

Chapter 4

Warren thought about riding over. Jumping on Coal, the Thoroughbred stallion he'd purchased several years ago when he was still a pony. Thought about kicking up dust and laying down grass, much like Charli had done when arriving at his place. He'd been impressed with her horsemanship and a part of him wanted to show her that she wasn't the only one who could sit in a saddle and handle business.

Warren had been riding horses since he could walk and of all of his brothers was the one most connected to the land. But he bypassed the stables and headed to the makeshift parking lot that when finished would be a circular design that could comfortably hold a dozen vehicles or more. He'd drive over, like most people would in the twenty-first century. *I'm not trying to impress her; no reason to.* This thought entered his mind as he opened the door to his cherry-red Maserati and slid inside.

After discussing it with his brother and Jackson, he'd

come up with an answer to his neighbor's problem. Not that he needed to, mind you. What happened on her land with her property was not his responsibility. No sirree, as his grandfather would say. And even though he'd be sure and keep mindful of the mile his father warned some would take for an inch of kindness, Warren also heeded his mother's words to "play nice" and his own desire to take a chance.

She sensed him first. Before seeing the dust, before hearing the car, Charli felt a squiggle go from her core to a place that had seen little action in the past two years. Rising from her kneeling position where she'd been pulling the weeds trying to get friendly with her kales and collards, she shielded her eyes from the midday sun and squinted. Rare for a car to be coming down this road and she wouldn't know who it was. But she did know. Could sense that it was him. One of them. One of the bourgie possums. Who else would drive such a swanky car in the middle of dirt roads, jackrabbits and tumbleweed?

"What does he want?" she mumbled, angrily pulling off her gardening gloves and trying to ignore the rapid beating of her heart. "He's the last person I want to see." *Liar!* She began walking to the road on slightly shaky legs, anger rising at the way her body reacted. He was just a man. Her farm was full of them. She'd grown up with them all around her. And now of all times she was growing moist between her legs? *Ridiculous.*

She reached the drive just as Warren turned off the engine. She stood there, arms crossed, face properly scowled to show the working of one's nerves. The nonchalant mask threatened to slip a bit as after a brief moment the man got out—translation: uncoiled—his long, lean frame from a car that looked too small to hold him. She'd refused to consider it yesterday but now allowed herself to guess. Around six-four. Or five. Around two hundred pounds. Probably five percent body fat. She tried to digest these thoughts with the disinterest of one examining cattle flesh. In that vein, this was a very nice bull.

When he first turned off the engine, Warren didn't move. He sat there fairly entranced at the vision before him. Backlit by the sun, she looked like an angel: a halo of long, unruly hair, skin bronzed and glowing, fitted white tee that unlike the oversize one she'd worn yesterday clung to her ample breasts and let him know that she was all woman. Her jeans were worn and tattered, clinging to curvy thighs, toned, no doubt, by the way she rode a horse. *She can probably clench them tight enough to crack a walnut.* Blood rushed to another nut, followed by thoughts of what else she could clench, causing Warren to shift his body and his thoughts while reaching for the door handle and finding a smile.

"Good afternoon." A curt nod was her greeting. "Nice-looking place you've got here." She cocked her head to the other side. Okay, so she wouldn't win the trophy for Miss Congeniality. Warren decided to bypass the small talk and get right to the point. "I, uh, think I might have an answer to the problem you mentioned yesterday."

She uncrossed her arms. "I'm listening."

With her arms now at her side, Warren found himself drawn once again to that rack of a body: full, round breasts, narrow waist, wide hips…*damn. Is it possible for her to look even better than she did yesterday?* She placed her hands in her back pockets and fixed him with a look that suggested she was long on agitation and short on patience.

"We can put a gate on that part of the fence, the part that's by the stream."

"Will it be locked?"

"Most likely. It's too far away for my men to oversee and while it's a good distance away from the vineyard, I don't want to have to wonder who or what might be sneaking through."

"So how is this giving access to my cattle?"

"Just tell me what time you need it open and I can make sure that happens."

"I don't appreciate having to give you a schedule."

"And I don't appreciate your funky attitude. Has anybody ever pointed it out to you?"

"A time or two."

It was a brief instant, a nanosecond really, but Warren could have sworn that the merest of smiles accompanied this statement. And he would be damned if he didn't kind of like it.

"We can install a gate and work out a time frame each day that it will be open and available to your livestock. That's my offer. Take it or leave it."

"I guess I'll take it, though it would be much easier if the gate remained unlocked. Other than coyote and deer there's not much to worry about around these parts. We had an issue with cow rustlers awhile back, but we fixed that problem."

"How'd you do that?"

"With a twenty-two."

"Ha!"

There it was again, that almost smile. He was sure he'd seen it this time.

"How soon can you get that gate in?"

"We'll order it today. As soon as it arrives, shouldn't take more than a day to have it installed."

Another nod.

"Well, I guess that's it."

He hesitated, having nothing more to say but not wanting to go. He'd had his share of women, even had one chomping at the bit to marry him. But there was something about this one, something about her feistiness and her don't-give-a-damn attitude that moved him, intrigued him, made him want to know about her and maybe break down that wall. It made him wonder about the man responsible for her building it in the first place. But none of this was his business. She was his neighbor, nothing more, and probably one he wouldn't see much past this meeting.

"All right then. Goodbye." He turned and headed back to his car, his long strides quickly widening the distance between them.

"Drake."

He turned back around. "The name's Warren." He said this even though he liked the way his surname rolled off her tongue. He liked the sound of her voice, too, low and raspy, could imagine it moaning in the throes of pleasure.

"Thank you. I appreciate it."

He smiled, got into his car and drove away, feeling as proud as a Boy Scout who'd just earned a new badge. He had a feeling there was a lot more to Charli Reed than met the eye. And in this moment, he silently admitted that he wanted to know it all.

Chapter 5

Warren parked his car next to Jackson's truck. There were also a few cars he didn't recognize.

Jackson looked up as he approached. "Must not have gone too bad."

"It went all right."

"No battle scars, head still intact, proof that she didn't bite it off."

Warren grinned. "She wanted to."

Richard walked up, having heard the last exchange. "A hellion, that one. I sure would like to tame her."

"You won't have time for that," Warren retorted, harsher than he'd intended. "I want this house finished as soon as possible, eight weeks tops. That includes the guest houses." He turned to Jackson. "Still think we can meet that deadline?"

"For the right price, anything is possible. Especially in this economy. There are plenty of men looking for work and workers love nothing better than overtime pay."

"I want you to get the size of crew you need to deliver within that time frame. Life will be easier if I'm living here during at least part of the harvesting of the first crop. Just run the numbers by me."

Jackson nodded. "Will do." He looked at Richard. "I left the roll of blueprints down by where the pool is going to be. Do you think you can go and bring it up for me?"

"Sure, man," Richard responded. He gave Warren a quick, unreadable look, then turned and left.

Jackson watched after him, his eyes narrowed in thought. "What's his story?"

"Richard is an old friend from New Orleans. Made some bad choices that landed him in prison. Our families are close—he became almost like a brother after my grandfather became his mentor. Practically lived at his home, became real close to my grandmother and later my mom. She talked me into helping him get a fresh start. Hard to land a job with a felony on your résumé."

"What'd he do?"

"Sold drugs. Made a lot of money, too. I think the feds took most of it."

"Easy come, easy go."

"Exactly."

"You trust him?"

Warren's head shot up. "Yes. Why?"

"I don't know. Something about his eyes."

"Richard is always running game, but he's cool overall."

Jackson's look showed he was not convinced. "You remember where I grew up, right? South Central L.A., where our playground was the streets. Brothers like him, who thought they were smarter, shrewder and more clever than the rest, were a dime a dozen and easy to spot. If I were you, I'd keep an eye out."

Warren nodded. "Think you'll have enough work to keep him busy?"

"I'll have enough work to keep his mind off of that fine filly who's got your nose wide open."

"Charli's easy on the eyes, I'll give her that. Not my type, though. Too mannish, too much attitude. I like women who enjoy being women, know what I'm saying?"

"Sure, War. If you say so."

"I say so," Warren said firmly, then quickly changed the subject. "Where's Diamond?"

"Probably buying up half of San Francisco. But I'd better get busy. She wants me to try out some swanky restaurant tonight. Our reservations are at eight and she threatened to hold out on the nooky if I'm late."

"Then by all means...let me leave you to your work."

Warren began walking toward the stables, noting that as Richard brought up the blueprints that Jackson wanted, he kept looking in the direction of Charli's place.

You trust him? Something about his eyes.

He'd given Jackson ready answers but in hindsight the question gave him pause. True, he'd known Richard for years, but people could change. He'd heard of more than one man who'd come back from prison a different man. So far, Richard acted like his old self. Warren would be paying close attention to make sure he stayed that way.

Chapter 6

"Miss Alice, I know you mean well, but—"

"No, no ifs, ands or buts, Charlene. I promised your grandfather that I'd watch over you, make sure you don't get swallowed up by that ranch. You're going to the dance."

Charli jumped up from the comfy rocker in the living room and began to pace the hardwood floors. "Let's do something else," she suggested, switching the phone to her other ear. "Go into the city for shopping or lunch."

"I've suggested that, remember? Two or three times. Hasn't happened."

"Next week, promise."

"The dance. Tonight." Amid Charli's continued sulking, Alice continued, "How can you even think about not attending the Days of Paradise Ball? This is the one time of year that all of the residents get together, the one time that we celebrate the founding of our town."

"I entered cattle in the farm animal contest."

"All well and good, but the dance is the main event. You've got to come."

"I don't have anything to wear!" It was Charli's long shot, banking on a short memory.

"Nonsense, you have that beautiful dress I ordered for you last month." So much for that hope. Alice's memory was fine. "You tried it on at my house, remember? It fit you perfectly."

"Miss Alice, you know how I feel about these types of events, and the people who will be attending."

"Yes, and it's high time you change those feelings. You can try and deny it as much as you want to but this is where you belong. Your mother—"

"Is she the one behind all this?" Charli stopped in her tracks. "Will she be there?"

"Charlene, I know you and your mother have had your share of differences." Charli let out an unladylike snort. "But she really does love you."

"Oh, really? Is that why she abandoned me for her lover? Is that why I spent so much time with Grandpa Charles growing up?"

"Did you not like spending time with Charles?"

"You know I loved Gramps. That's not the point."

"I hope you can resolve these feelings of ill will, child. Pierre is now your stepfather."

"That man will *never* be *anything* to me."

"Your mother will not be there, Charlene."

"I wish you'd call me Charli."

"Charlene is a beautiful name for a beautiful woman. It's that feminine side of you that gets far too little attention. I want you to let her out tonight. With me. At the dance."

Charli sighed. "You're just not going to quit bugging me, are you?"

"Sure I will. Just as soon as you get here. Say, around seven?"

"What time does the party start?"

"Nine. But you need time to get ready."

"How long does it take to put on a dress?"

"We need our girl time. I have someone coming over for our hair and makeup. See you in about two hours?"

"If you insist."

"I do."

Warren stood in the middle of his walk-in closet, staring at what he called his monkey suits and wishing for the umpteenth time that he hadn't picked up the phone. He recalled the conversation.

"I had other plans for tonight, Mother."

That those plans were a delivered pizza and early bedtime need not be shared.

"I reminded you about the table for ten we purchased two weeks ago," his mother had countered. "You promised you'd come."

"I don't remember."

"You were on your way out the door. But you agreed."

"Great."

"The money made from the sale of tables is for a good cause. We're going to build a combination food bank and donation center somewhere in town. Everyone goes to the Days of Paradise gala, Warren. Besides, you've been working too hard lately. And there's a surprise."

Oh, here we go. "Who is she?"

He grimaced at his mother's tinkling chuckle, grating because of what was sure to come next.

"Rachel's home."

"So now we get to the real reason for all this prodding."

"Surprised you need it for such a beautiful girl, or rather, young woman. She's even more stunning than when she left to finish her senior year. You're almost thirty years old, Warren. Time to think about settling down."

"Junior's thirty-two. Go and bug him."

"Oh, trust me, Ike Jr. gets his share of…encouragement. But right now I'm not talking to him. I'm talking to you." Silence. "Rachel graduated with dual degrees in psychology and music theory."

"She's still playing the piano?"

"Beautifully, even participated in a concert at Carnegie Hall. Any man would be blessed to have her. She's gorgeous, talented, comes from a great family with morals like ours."

"And it doesn't hurt that her father works for the leader of the free world."

"I'd never want to be considered a social climber, but yes, her father's prestigious position at the White House is a definite plus."

"Which tux should I wear, black, navy or gray?"

"The black one, definitely. And it would be a nice touch, sweetheart, if you brought Rachel a little welcome-home gift. Nothing too frilly. A single rose, perhaps? Or a nice box of chocolates?"

"I'd rather not, Mother. I know how women think and to give her anything like that would be giving her the wrong idea."

"You're a kind, thoughtful man, no? What's wrong about that?"

"Absolutely nothing. Which is why I'll welcome Rachel home with a greeting and a smile."

"Now, Warren—"

"Goodbye, Mother. See you at the dance."

He finished dressing, splashed on cologne and headed for the door. A smile spread across his face as a thought occurred. He'd told his mother that he was coming to the dance. But he hadn't told her how long he planned to stay. Not long. He felt better already.

Chapter 7

Anybody entering the Paradise Cove Country Club would be hard-pressed to imagine it belonged to a community of less than three thousand. Every aspect of the building was magnificent, both inside and out, and everyone who entered the solid brass double doors looked as though they belonged. Limos vied with Maybachs and Bentleys and enough diamonds sparkled to rival the night's starry sky.

"Warren!"

He turned around and smiled as the twins walked toward him. "Hello, Teresa." He leaned down to give his sister a hug. "You look amazing."

She curtsied. "Well, thank you, brother dear. You look dapper as well."

"Terrell." Warren and his brother shared a fist bump and a hug.

"Careful," Terrell said, brushing nonexistent lint off each of his shoulders. "Don't mess up the threads."

"Trouble coming toward us," Teresa mumbled, turning her head and twirling a curl.

Warren resisted looking, but Terrell turned around. "Well, if it isn't Mr. CEO and the princess."

Now he didn't have to turn around. He knew who it was: Ms. Gold Digger, Ms. Social Climber. Ms. Will Do Anything to Marry a Drake. Niko had alluded to bringing someone respectable. Even though her stint as an exotic dancer had been very brief and in another state, Terrell knew that this was not the title his mom would give Ashley. She was going to be furious.

"Hello, family," Niko said as he approached.

"Hello, Niko," Warren said with a brother's handshake. "Ashley," he said with a nod.

"Hello, everyone," Ashley responded.

"Where's the rest of the family?" Niko asked.

"Inside," Warren said, "and they're probably wondering about us. Let's go join them."

The Drakes entered and the response they received resembled the Red Sea parting. Everyone turned and those in their path stepped back, offering hugs, greetings and compliments as they made their way to the table where their parents and remaining siblings either sat or stood chatting.

There was someone else there, too. Rachel.

"There you are!" Jennifer waved Warren over as soon as she saw him.

His mother was right. Rachel was stunning. She looked like a tanned porcelain doll—perfect and delicate—her hair designed in attractive ringlets, her beaded dress a perfect fit, her jewelry, which he knew cost a mint, elegant and understated. So why in this moment did his mind drift to a surly neighbor with dirty hands and scuffed boots?

"Hello, Rachel." He leaned in to give her a light hug.

She wrapped her arms around his neck for a longer, more personal squeeze. "Warren," she said, stepping back but continuing to hold his hand. "It is so great to see you. Now I really feel like I'm home."

"Rachel has agreed to join the Golden Gates auxiliary and help with the plans to raise money for the center I told you about, and a variety of other charities."

"That's wonderful."

"There are so many unfortunate people in this world," Rachel stated, long, thick lashes surrounding the doe-like eyes that looked at Warren in a love-starved way. "It's the least I can do."

"You've always been such a caring soul, Rachel. I think that…" In a rare moment, Jennifer was distracted to the point that she lost her train of thought. "Who is that with Alice?" she asked, as if to herself.

Warren and Rachel followed the direction of Jennifer's gaze.

"I'm not sure," Rachel responded.

Warren said nothing. Couldn't, he was speechless. Because he knew exactly who it was, and he couldn't believe it.

Charli had one single goal for the night: get through it without falling flat on her butt. How women walked, even danced, in heels was beyond her. And panty hose? Geez. Now she had an idea how ground pork felt in casing. The makeup was foreign on her face; she had to constantly squelch the urge to rub it off. The only thing about Alice's forced makeover that felt remotely comfortable was the hairstyle. She liked it up and away from her face. But she'd trade all the sparkly pins for a scrunchie in a New York minute.

"I'd like to think all of the gentlemen are looking this way because of my new 'do," Alice said, patting her freshly cut silver bob. "But it's clear who's caught their eye."

Charli wished it wasn't. Being the center of attention

wasn't her forte unless the surrounding crowd came with four legs and a snout. "I wish they'd quit staring. It's disconcerting."

"By the look on some of the women's faces," Alice said, eyes gleaming, "you aren't the only one unnerved. I see some of my friends, darling. Come."

Halfway to their destination it happened again. She felt him. Strongly. Without a shadow of a doubt she knew that Warren Drake was here. *Keep walking, Charli. And don't fall!*

"Warren, are you listening?"

"Sorry, Rachel. What did you say?"

"Never mind. It's clear your attention is elsewhere."

"I've been following you mostly, and am impressed that you want to use your degree to, you know…"

"Follow weather patterns."

"Right."

"Wrong, Warren! You're not listening at all." Rachel's normally placid face was in full pout. "You haven't heard a word anyone has said since *she* walked in."

"Who?"

"Do you know her?"

"Not really."

"Well, now's your chance." She walked off in a huff.

Clearly, she was perturbed. With good reason. He was acting like a love-struck fool. "Rachel!"

She didn't stop. He started to follow her, and then thought better of that idea. *Best to let her cool off* was his first thought. *Maybe I'll get those flowers or chocolates after all,* his second. And his third? To make his way over to the reason for Rachel's frustration. He turned to do so, took two steps and watched as Richard strolled up to Charli. He took her hand and raised it for a gentlemanly kiss. Always the suave one, that Richard, what with the flawless, smooth face, soft curly locks and bedroom eyes framed by girlishly long lashes. He'd been turning on the charm since grade school and at the beginning of college could pull any girl he wanted away from Warren's once-clumsy clutches.

But Warren was no longer clumsy and this was not college. Lips set in a determined line, he once again prepared to cross the room. And stopped. *Wait a minute.* A scene played in his mind: him driving over to Charli's house with news about the gate; Charli's less than amicable response. All right, it had been downright chilly. His question about her snarly attitude. Her answer that she both knew about it and was not apologetic. She would probably rip Richard a new one in less than thirty ticks. Grinning, Warren took a glass of champagne from a floating waiter, became partially hidden as he leaned against the wall next to a large potted plant and prepared to watch the show.

It was not what he expected.

Where was that perpetual scowl she'd exhibited, the crossed arms and narrowed eyes? As Richard took her hand Charli smiled, actually *smiled.* Was it indeed possible for her to enjoy herself? This Warren would have doubted just one short day ago. But no, there it was: easy, impish and beautiful—straight white teeth and sparkling eyes. Richard said something to her. She tossed back her head in laughter, which brought Warren's attention to that long, graceful neck, the one that had invaded his thoughts with more frequency than he'd desired, along with the things he wanted to do to said neck before moving on to other equally tantalizing body parts. He drank her much as he did the champagne and imagined she tasted the same: full-bodied, robust with hints of floral notes and spices. Amazing that this mesmerizingly pretty creature wrapped in silk was the same one he'd observed pulling weeds in tattered denim. Among this posh and polished crowd, she looked as though she belonged. *Just who are you, Charli Reed?*

"Pulling recognizance?" Niko drawled as he sidled up to his preoccupied sib.

Warren forced his eyes away from Charli, actually turned his back on the way-too-cozy scene and answered his brother. "She's my neighbor. Quite the sourpuss when I met her. I actually thought Richard was getting ready to get dismissed, but old girl surprised me. They're getting along."

"I guess Richard still has the juice?"

Warren didn't mean to scowl, but his face didn't get the memo.

"You have a problem with that?"

"As a matter of fact, I do."

"What are you going to do about it?"

"I'm going to break up their little tête-à-tête and grab this next dance."

Chapter 8

On his way over, Warren watched Richard say something to Charli and then head over to the bar, presumably to get drinks.

Perfect timing, my man.

Warren circled around and purposely came up behind Charli, leaving her no time to don a surly mask. "May I have this dance?"

"Do you want to dance—" Charli looked down at Warren's hold on her "—or arm wrestle?" The smile was still there but her eyes showed fire. "That's a pretty tight grip."

He loosened it, but didn't release her. "You look to be the type who can handle it."

"Kindly let me go," she demanded.

"*Kindly* let me have this dance."

Charli was just about to jerk away from him when she saw Alice heading their way, with someone she despised even more than the Drakes.

"Charlene!" Alice stopped, her arm looped around the

arm of the man who accompanied her. "Look who I spotted just as he was entering the room."

The man reached for Charli's hand. "Hello, beautiful."

She tucked it behind her and stepped closer to Warren. "Hi, Cedric."

"It's been a long time, Charlene. You look good."

"Miss Alice, if you'll excuse us. We were just heading to the dance floor."

Once in the throng of dancers swaying to the smooth, soulful sounds of a song about distant lovers, Warren quickly wrapped his arms around Charli's waist. He was assaulted by many things at once: the smell of perfume, the softness of silk and the feel of this woman's body next to his own. She felt so right. With her in heels, her temple brushed his chin. If she turned and tilted her head oh so slightly the kiss would be right there. Hot, he imagined. Long, he'd make sure. There was only word for it: heaven. So much so that he was tempted to ignore the reason this morsel had wound up in his arms. But he didn't.

"Ex-boyfriend?"

"No."

"Ex-lover?"

"Can we just dance?"

"Certainly." With the fluidity of one trained in this art, Warren took Charli's left hand in his right, even as he gently yet firmly pressed her flush against him. "Just follow my lead," he whispered in her ear. With that he spun them around, swaying smoothly to the beat. He rubbed his thumb across the small of her back, eased his hand precariously close to Charli's firm, round booty. Close enough to feel the curve, far enough to still be a gentleman. Barely.

She tried to focus elsewhere: on the decor, the music (though Marvin Gaye seriously was not helping matters), even the bouffant hairdo on the town's matriarch, Mrs.

Gentry. But nothing was proving distracting. Warren's presence was all-consuming—from his hard chest to his dance moves, from his cologne to the vibration from his chest as he hummed the song. When he pulled her into his arms, her knees had almost buckled. Even now, only sheer willpower prevented her from melting into his powerful frame, teasing the hair at the nape of his neck and resting her forehead against his strong jaw. It had been a long time since she'd felt safe enough to relax, let her guard down, live without worry. Being with someone like Warren could help her feel that way.

Except being with Warren wasn't a possibility. Ever.

"Is that guy a problem?"

She could feel the strength in his chest as he spoke. God, what that deep voice did to parts of her soul! But it did something else. It took her out of her musings and brought her crashing back down to the reality of where she was and why. Dancing had given her a temporary reprieve from the man she would have been altogether peachy with never seeing again in life. But sooner or later she knew she'd have to deal with Cedric. She told herself there was no fear there, but shivered nonetheless.

The song ended. Warren stepped back, his hands on her arms, his eyes boring into her. "Charli, are you all right?"

"I can take care of myself," she replied with a defiant lift of her chin.

"That's not what I asked you."

For an awkward moment they stood there, something indefinable yet palpable passing between them. Another song started, this one upbeat, and soon more couples swirled around them.

"Thanks for the dance," he said with one last squeeze of her arm. And then he was gone.

If he'd waited a second more he would have seen that Charli didn't stay alone for long. She felt a lone finger

run down her bare back and wheeled around. "Stop it!"
I should have known he'd hound me. "Look, Cedric. I
don't want any trouble out of you. I just want you to leave
me alone."

"Or what?" Cedric looked around. "Is that your boyfriend? He doesn't scare me."

"I'm no longer that little girl that you cornered in the
barn," Charli said with a sneer, as rising memories pushed
her past the point of worrying about decorum or caring
for her safety. "The friend who'll keep me safe from you
isn't walking on two legs."

"Oh, you have a guard dog? I'm scared." He faked a
shudder.

"You should be." Charli's voice was low, her smile men-
acing. "Because I believe in the Second Amendment, and
if you come near me again my guard dog—" she looked
loathingly up and down Cedric's five-nine frame "—will
have no problem relieving you of your family jewels. I'm
sure they're so small that shooting them may be difficult.
But I'm a pretty good aim."

With that, Charli calmly walked away.

Two pairs of eyes followed her over to the table, where
she joined the woman who Warren had learned from his
mother was named Alice Witherspoon.

Niko looked at his brother. "Looks like your neighbor
might be in trouble."

Warren took a sip of his drink, watching as Cedric exited the building. "I'm not worried about Charli. I think
she can hold her own."

Chapter 9

As it was harvesting season for their first yield of grapes, the week following the town of Paradise Cove's celebration went by in a blur. Warren had his hands full, his attention going from the crash course on grapes he was getting from his cousin Dexter Drake to checking the progress on his dream home that Jackson was building. There weren't enough hours in the day. He was exhausted, and at times had to remind himself that this was a madness he'd created.

"Hey, cuz." Warren walked up to his cousin Dexter, who was standing in one of the vineyard rows, talking to the manager.

Dexter turned to him. "Perfect timing, Warren. I was just suggesting to Eduardo that since all of the table grapes have been gathered these grapes, the chenin blancs, should be harvested next."

"Whatever you say, Dexter. I'm here to follow your lead and learn all that I can."

"Eduardo here is highly knowledgeable. For years his

father managed a large vineyard just down the road from ours. He's a wine country son through and through. Instead of milk, they put grape juice in your bottle, huh, Eduardo?"

"No," Eduardo replied, his dark eyes twinkling. "Wine."

The Drakes laughed.

"I think you've got a stellar crop here," Dexter continued, picking a grape and examining it closely: skin, pulp, seeds and all. "I know it's been a long time coming—"

"Five years," Warren interjected.

"But I think the wait will be well worth it."

"I couldn't have done any of this without your expertise, Dex."

"I'm just glad that you followed my advice and planted grapes instead of marijuana."

"Hey, don't knock that hustle! The medical marijuana business is booming. Weed is the number-one California crop!"

"Yes, but can you imagine the money you'd have had to spend on security? There are guys who'd want that crop, and they'd have no interest in turning it over to doctors and dispensaries."

"What really sealed it for me was all of the regulatory guidelines and bureaucratic red tape I would have had to deal with in getting the product into those authorized distribution channels. It would have been a nightmare. With my grapevines, I just have to pick up the phone, call you down from your throne in Southern California and have you oversee and execute the hard stuff."

"Ha! I'm afraid that's not how it works!"

"No?"

"I hope you're paying attention to these lessons I'm teaching. Because next year it's all on you."

"Come on, now, Dex! I—" His phone rang. "Oh, hold on. It's Jackson." He tapped the cell phone screen. "Hey, Boss." He paused, listening. "Oh, okay. Sure, I'll be right over." He ended the call. "The gate has come in," he said to Dexter and Eduardo. "I need to go down to where the men will be installing it."

"No worries, Warren. Eduardo and I will have a short meeting with the workers and that will pretty much wrap up my visit."

"I appreciate it, man." Warren gave Dexter a shoulder-bump hug. "If you'd like, you're welcome over to Mom's house for dinner. As always."

"I'd love to but I've already booked a flight back to San Diego. Faye says little David has a bit of a fever. So I'm going to go on back and help her out."

"The doctor tamed the playboy. Who would have ever imagined Dexter Drake would pass up a Friday night in San Francisco for a night with a wife and a kid's spittle?"

"Don't knock it until you try it," Dexter replied.

"That's what *you* did!"

"You're right. I thought a wife and children were for other people and that my role in life was to be the cool uncle who spoiled nieces and nephews before sending them back home."

"All kidding aside, I hope your son will be okay."

"I'm sure he will."

"Okay, Dex. I need to run. Give Faye my love."

"Will do."

The two men shared a final handshake before Warren turned and left.

After a short ride in the golf cart—another of Dexter's suggestions—Warren arrived at the section of the fence in the area described as the "south forty." There were four crewmen there, one wearing a gray shirt with the logo of the company that had sold Warren the gate. The gate and corresponding hardware had been unloaded and the workers were arranging the pieces on the ground.

Warren walked over to the man sporting the company logo and held out his hand. "Warren Drake."

"Steve Humphries," the man replied, his grip firm, his scruffy day-old beard showing wisps of gray that belied his boyishly good looks. "I thought we'd make the opening there," he said, pointing to where one of the men had a measuring tape, marking off the fence in two places. "Would you prefer that the gate swings inward or out?"

"Which do you suggest?"

Steve looked at the fence and at the land beyond it. "How will the gate be used?"

"The neighbor has cattle that will be coming in to drink at the stream, just over that ridge."

"In that case, I think swinging inward would be most beneficial. Are there a lot of cattle?"

Warren squinted, recalling past conversations with Charli. Then he looked at Steve. "That's a good question." He retrieved his cell phone. "Shoot, I don't have her phone number. Do you need this information to get started?"

"No. But I do need to explain the automatic lock system and how it can be activated and deactivated, even from a remote location."

After receiving a crash course on operating the gate, Warren drove the cart to where his car was parked but on second thought, continued past it to the stables. He jumped out and went over to where one of the workers was grooming Coal, his pride and joy.

"Hello, Mr. Warren."

"Hello, Anthony."

"Want me to saddle him up, sir?"

"No, I'll handle it. You can finish feeding the other horses and then clean out their stalls."

He walked over to the majestic black stallion, who immediately began bowing his head in greeting.

"Hello, Coal," Warren said, his voice low and soothing as he stroked the lustrous mane of the proud beast. "It's time to go and visit a pretty lady. Ready to go for a ride?"

Chapter 10

As he rounded the bend in the road leading up to the Reed ranch house, Warren sat straighter in the saddle, for the first time wishing he'd forgone his favorite Raider ball cap for the Stetson he'd purchased a few years ago but seldom wore. The blazing sun overhead was only partly the reason. There was something about his prickly neighbor that made him want to cowboy up, in more ways than one. Not that he was trying to impress her or anything.

No, never that.

He neared the wooden gate surrounding the property and looked at the garden beyond it. No sign of her. The area around the barn, stables and detached garage was equally quiet. He reached the fence, dismounted and looped the horse's reins over a post. He removed his cap, wiped the sweat from his brow and knocked on the door.

A wiry man who looked to be anywhere from sixty-something to as old as God came to the door. Although it was warm he wore heavy denims and a flannel shirt.

There was a stained white apron tied around his middle, a kerchief at his throat and a toothpick clenched between his teeth. Warren imagined that the man could have ridden with the great Bill Pickett, perhaps even been related.

The man opened the door, sharp, white eyes peering out of his weathered face. "Afternoon."

"Afternoon, sir. Is Charli here?"

The eyes narrowed. "Who wants to know?"

"Oh, I'm sorry. Warren," he replied, holding out his hand. "Warren Drake. I own the ranch and vineyard just down the road." He clasped a hand that felt like steady work and hard living. "And you are?"

"Griff."

"Griff? Nice to meet you. Is Griff your first name or your last name?"

The toothpick moved from one side of Griff's mouth to the other. "Yep."

"Okay." *Clearly you are where Charli learned her good manners.* Feeling that voicing this thought was not the best course of action, Warren decided upon another approach. "I have some news for her regarding her cattle, and the stream that's on my land. She's been waiting for an update. Is she here?"

Griff removed the toothpick from his mouth, raising his head a notch as he eyed Warren. "You Walter's kin?"

"I am." Warren smiled, unconsciously lifting his chin with pride. "He's my grandfather. Do you know him?"

The toothpick returned to its place of prominence between the teeth. "We've met a time or two."

"Was it during the time that he and Charles Reed were partners?"

Griff stepped out onto the porch, walked past Warren, and shot a perfect stream of tobacco juice into a hydrangea bush. "That's a fine piece of horseflesh."

"My pride and joy." Warren joined Griff at the edge of the porch, standing by his side to admire the animal.

"Thoroughbred?"

"Arabian."

"Can you ride him bareback?"

"I can ride any horse, saddle or not."

Griff shot him a skeptical look before turning back toward the house. When he reached the door he placed his hand on the latch, then said without turning back around, "She's out in the pasture, with the cowhands. Best to state your business and be gone."

The sound of horse hooves pounding the earth drew Charli's attention from the injured cow. She turned her head toward the sound, shielding her eyes to try to make out the rider. Over the years, she'd become so attuned to each horse and the worker who rode it that she usually knew who approached her without having to look. But not this time. The hoofbeats were too heavy and too rapid to belong to Griff and his horse, Danger. They were too authoritative to be that of cowhand Willie and his horse, Shaft. The only other workers here today were the two now with her, which meant one thing. There was a stranger on her land.

She stood, dusting off her jeans as the commanding rider came into view. A familiar feeling danced over her, but she ignored it. *No way. The only horsepower he's used to is under a hood.* At once, she recognized both the quality of the horse and the skill of the rider. As they came closer, she noticed something else. The broad, hard shoulders that had occupied way too many of this week's errant thoughts. The jutting chin and strong neck from which she'd smelled a cologne that matched its wearer—striking and bold.

It's him.

She swallowed and willed herself to remain detached, demanded her body not to react and her stance not to waver. But not trusting her hands to behave themselves once he got within touching distance, she stooped back down to tend to the injured cow.

Warren reached the small group and climbed off the horse. He joined them. "Hello, Charli."

"Drake," she responded without looking up.

"What happened?" he asked, kneeling beside her.

That damnable cologne hit her nostrils at once, bringing back the memories of that night, their dance, into clearer focus. She could almost feel his hands—one clasping her own, the other hovering just above her round assets—could almost feel his breath against her neck.

She stood abruptly, walked over to her horse and pulled a cell phone from her saddlebag. Yes, she needed to make a call, but even more so, she needed to put some distance between herself and *that man.* "More than likely hit a plug in the dirt at the exact wrong angle," she finally answered while scrolling through the names showing on the phone's screen. "Looks like her leg's broken." She looked at one of the cowhands. He was a serious-looking young man with a slender build, his high cheekbones, hawk nose and long, silky black hair bound in a ponytail an obvious result of his Native American heritage. "Bobby, I was going to call Jim. Have him bring over the floating tank. Just on the small chance that it's merely sprained."

"No," Bobby said, shaking his head. He knelt and placed a hand on the cow's heaving side. The animal breathed slowly, steadily, as if resigned to its fate. "There is no hope for this animal." He looked at Charli. "Do you want me to—"

"No," Charli said, cutting him off with the soft yet firmly delivered word. "You know how we do it out here, Bobby. My cow, my kill." Once again she walked over to her horse, this time taking a .22-gauge rifle from out of a saddle holder. She walked back over to the cow. "Bobby?"

The young man, who was still kneeling, leaned forward as if whispering in the cow's ear. Then he stood and said something in a language that Warren did not understand. Judging from everyone's silence, and the way the air felt around him, he would have guessed it was a prayer. Charli stepped up, the men moved back and she fired. One clean shot. Between the eyes. The cow was dead.

While the cowhands tended to the animal, Charli walked back over to her horse. Warren followed her. "What do you want, Drake?" she asked, placing the gun back in its holder.

He decided to ignore her attitude for the moment. After all, the woman had just shot a cow. "I came over to let you know that the gate arrived. The men are installing it now. It is electronic, opened by a code that gets entered into a box on a nearby post. In case of a power outage, it can also be opened manually. I wanted to give you both the code and a key."

She looked down at the big silver key in the palm of his large hand, and back up at him. "You'd trust me with a key inside the Drake domain?"

"You can't be trusted?"

"Of course I can! We Reeds keep our word."

"Meaning…"

She shrugged, said, "Nothing," and reached for the key.

Warren closed his fist. Patience was gone. "Not so fast. I've put up with your rude behavior and foul attitude long enough. I go to your house and get more veiled jabs and hidden innuendo from First-and-Last-Name-Griff." He took a step forward, close enough that their breath mingled and their bodies almost touched. "If you have a problem with me or my family," he continued, his tone low and angry, "tell me straight out. If you don't, then you need to start treating me with at least as much respect as you just gave that cow."

Chapter 11

Bobby's footsteps had been so light that neither Warren nor Charli had heard him approaching. "Everything all right here, Charli?" The question was directed at his boss but his eyes were on Warren.

"Everything's fine, Bobby. Thanks for your help. Listen, the cowhide's yours if you want it."

"Thank you, Charli. I'll give it to my uncle. He'll make something special."

"I'm sure he will." She turned to Warren—her gaze unwavering, her eyes sending a message that he couldn't quite read. "Where are you putting the gate?"

"Close to the southwest corner, where the land is flat and the path is worn from the obvious trips back and forth to the stream over the years. Would you like to come and have a look?"

She hesitated slightly before giving a curt nod, slipping a foot into the stirrup and swinging up onto her mount. "Tell Griff I'll be back in time for supper," she said to the men, then turned her horse toward Drake's place, touched its flanks with her feet and raced across the terrain without looking back.

Oh, really? That's how you do it? That's how you want to get down? The somber events Warren had just witnessed receded as he watched Charli run away. He was up on his horse and they moved in one fluid motion.

"Yah!"

He eased up on the reins, applying gentle pressure to Coal's sides with his thighs and calves. Coal lunged forward, dirt churning beneath his powerful strides. Charli was an exceptional rider. This he knew. He also respected the beautiful palomino that she rode, admired its smooth gait and steely determination. Perhaps this was why he held Coal back just enough to keep her hopes up, just enough to let her believe that there might actually be a chance that she'd win. But when the fence to his property came into view about a hundred yards away, he leaned forward, applied the slightest pressure to the horse's sides with his thighs and uttered a simple command: "Go!"

Coal did just that. Raising his head as if sensing the wind and his owner's desire to win, the horse bolted forward in long, smooth strides. His front legs curled back and his back legs reached forward in a choreographed movement that for anyone watching was a sight to behold. It took Warren fifty yards to catch her, ten yards for them to exchange glances (his of confidence, hers of resignation mixed with chagrin), and forty yards to finish the impromptu race, both slowing down their mounts as they neared the fence. The gate had been installed and the men had left. Warren reached it first, pulling Coal's reins to the left and leading the horse in a wide semicircle for a quick cooldown.

"Good boy," he whispered to the majestic creature, rubbing his mane as he did so. "Whoa, boy, we're done for now," he added, when the horse kept prancing even after he pulled the reins.

After cooling down her mount in a similar fashion, Charli rode up beside Warren. "That's a beautiful horse."

"Thank you."

"Racehorse?"

"They're often used as such. I've bred him with a couple mares whose owners have that goal."

"I didn't know that you were a horseman."

"There are a lot of things about me that you don't know."

Their eyes locked and held, even as both of their animals tossed their manes as though engaged as well in conversation.

"You were right back there. I've been rude. I apologize."

He removed his sunglasses, looked her squarely in the eye and saw sincerity, among other less definable emotions. "I accept it."

A myriad of questions whirled around in Warren's head but something told him now was not the time to ask them. Instead, he dismounted and walked over to the fence post between the fence and gate joints. There was a small box attached to the top of it with a number pad displayed. Warren keyed in the four-digit access code he'd created and the gates eased open.

"Nice," she said, passing by him and walking to the gate. Her hands ran lightly over the steel as she checked out the installation and mechanics. "Looks expensive."

"I believe in paying for quality when it's warranted. When it comes to this ranch I only install the best."

She looked at him. "You didn't have to put in this gate. I really do appreciate it."

He nodded even as he took in the sheen on her skin and the curve of her neck. The temperature was in the seventies, but like Griff, Charli wore a red plaid flannel shirt and Levi's. The scuffed boots were the ones he'd seen her in last week. Obviously her favorites. She shifted and at that moment the sun caught the jewels in her ear, bringing to Warren's attention that she wore earrings. They were bright red stones, with a dangling gold chain sporting an identical red stone on the end. They were dainty and feminine and seemingly incongruent with the tough veneer Charli chose to portray. It hinted at a softer, vulnerable side, Warren thought. The side he'd seen in her eyes just before she shot the cow, and last week at the dance, when the man had approached with her aunt. Each thought brought more questions, exposed more layers to this woman before him. Layers that intrigued him. Layers that he wanted to examine, learn why they were there and then help peel away.

"What did he say back there?"

Charli's head shot up. "What? Who?"

"Your worker. Before you shot the cow. What did he say?"

"Oh, Bobby. He offered a prayer for the life of the animal, sending its spirit back to where it began and thanking the earth for the sustenance that will now be ours through the animal's unavoidable sacrifice."

"Do you lose a lot of animals that way?"

"Not many."

"I could tell it wasn't easy, but you steeled yourself and did what you had to do."

"Comes with the territory."

"I could also tell that that wasn't your first time with a gun. Remind me not to ever become your target."

"I'd say you're safe, neighbor. For now." There it was again. That almost smile, more of a smirk, really, that he'd seen blossom across her face on occasion. Once she realized it was showing, that joy had been let loose, she hid it away.

He walked toward her, reaching into his pocket. "In that case…" He pulled out the gate key that he'd offered ear-

lier. She reached for it and when she touched his hand…
as had happened before…their world shifted.

She would have pulled away, but he enveloped her small
hand inside his much larger one, his almost black orbs boring into her lighter brown ones. His finger rubbed across
her wrist, and he felt her rapid pulse. It reminded Warren
of a summer in New Orleans, when he'd found and cornered a small rabbit in his grandfather's barn. The rabbit
had cowered in the corner, eyes wide with alarm, body
shivering from fear. Warren remembered feeling bad that
the hare was so afraid. He'd felt like the big bad wolf and
while some of his friends would have relished ending its
life, he'd wanted to make the rabbit feel safe, to let it know
that everything would be all right.

Charli was now that bunny that he wanted to reas-
sure. So as he'd done that summer when he was twelve he
began to soothe Charli. Slowly, methodically, he rubbed
his thumb back and forth across her wrist, finally releas-
ing her hand and sliding his up her arm. His pressure was
light, reassuring. He purposely avoided eye contact, fo-
cusing on his hand and her skin.

He felt her shiver and since the sun beamed down on
them both, knew it was not from cold. Without a word,
he took her in his arms. She was stiff at first, but as he
rubbed his hand over her shoulders and across her back
she relaxed, placed her arms around him and rested her
head against his chest.

Warren sensed that something somewhere inside her—
the tiniest edge of one of her layers—had just separated
from the staunch shell of the survivalist ego to which it
was attached, and was starting to peel.

While Warren was busy sensing all that was happening with Charli, there was something that he was missing.

That something inside himself was also shifting, a movement so subtle yet so significant that it would change both of their lives…and others', too.

Chapter 12

When was the last time that she'd felt this way? Safe. Protected. Beloved. She couldn't remember. Oh, yes, she could. Last weekend. At the dance. She closed her eyes and took a deep breath. His body soothed her. She could feel her shoulders relax, could imagine the coil of tension that was almost always in the pit of her stomach starting to unwind.

Then other feelings in other places started to emerge. Tender feelings, womanly feelings, that hadn't been stirred up since two years ago when life, with the help of her then fiancé, taught her that men were not to be trusted. The only man she'd believed in and who hadn't let her down was her grandfather. And Griff. So at least two men of their word had walked the earth.

Grandpa. Yes, those times with him I felt safe and secure. My head against his chest as we both lay on the afghan-covered sofa, watching reruns of Bonanza. *But*

Grandpa's gone. And I'm here with…a Drake…a relative of the man that Pa despised!

Charli jerked away from Warren and stumbled out of his embrace.

"Charli!" Warren reached to grab her but she held up her hand. "Charli, it's okay."

"No, it isn't. I lost myself for a moment. It's been a long and…trying day." She looked at him with wide, bright eyes, took a deep, calming breath and replaced this look with one of control. "Thanks again for everything."

Warren hadn't missed the emotional shifts: from calm and authentic to being fake and resigned. But as an astute businessman and an intuitive human, he knew how to play the game as well as she. He reached into his shirt pocket. "Here, I want to give you this."

Charli crossed her arms in front of her. "What's that?"

"My cell phone number."

"And I need it because…?"

"Um, because phones tend to be more reliable than smoke signals."

Her look said she wasn't buying it.

"It's the twenty-first century. We're neighbors. A phone call is faster than horsepower…or a ride on a horse, like what I had to do when my worker asked a simple question about how many cattle would be drinking at the stream. Turns out he didn't need the answer to finish the job, but it still made me realize having each other's number might come in handy."

Cynicism continued to trump common sense.

"As independent as you are, there might come a day when you find that you need someone outside your circle. Someone close by. A neighbor. That would be me."

When she replaced the look of disbelief with a blank stare, Warren walked over to her horse, placed the business card containing his cell phone number into her saddlebag and mounted his horse. This time it was he who rode away without a backward glance.

He reached the stables. It appeared that all of the construction workers were gone. He walked Coal inside, took off the saddle and rubbed him down. Coal's ears pricked up in alert just before Warren heard the crunch of gravel.

He turned around. "Richard. Where are you coming from? I thought everyone was gone."

Richard pulled off his sunglasses as he entered the stables. "I told Jackson's superintendent that I'd finish stacking up the rest of the wood they delivered this afternoon. Man, you're building a mansion. This place is going to be huge!"

"You think so?"

"If the amount of wood we're using is any indication, it's definitely going to be one of the biggest houses I've ever seen."

"So how is this job working out for you, Richard?"

Richard walked over to Coal, who reared away from him when he reached out to pet his mane, and seemed to look at him with a skeptical eye. "Okay, dude. Guess you don't want to be petted." He looked at Warren. "It's a job. But through this process I'm learning that I'm not really cut out for manual labor."

"I hear you, Rich. But I guess we all can handle anything for six or seven weeks, right?"

"I guess."

Knowing that the stable hand had seen him return and would finish wiping down the horse, clean the stall and spread feed later, Warren threw a few pitchforks full of fresh hay into Coal's stall and made sure there was a good amount of water in the trough. Then he headed out.

Richard followed him. "But I think this is going to be my first and only construction job."

They reached the temporary parking area, where Warren now noticed a truck parked next to his car. Upon closer inspection, he realized it belonged to Anthony, the stable hand. The car that Richard proudly drove, a classic, fully restored and customized 1972 Cadillac Eldorado, was parked farther down the drive.

"So how soon after the house is completed do you plan on returning to New Orleans?"

"I'm not sure I'll be going back."

"Really?" Warren ran his hand down the smooth lines of Richard's classic ride. Not one for old cars himself, he still admired how this one had been restored and how clean Richard kept it. Upon first seeing the car Warren had wondered how a newly released felon had been able to purchase and restore such a vehicle. But his mother had assured him it was all aboveboard. "He worked temporarily at a Cadillac dealership and became friends with the owner," she'd said. But then he'd become even friendlier with the owner's blonde-haired, blue-eyed daughter and that was when he'd no longer been welcome at the used-car lot.

"I like California," Richard said. "The weather is nice and the women are classy. Especially that neighbor of yours."

This got Warren's attention—immediately.

"When have you seen her? Except for the one time she came over about the fence?"

"A brother gets around," was Richard's vague answer.

Warren tried to keep his face blank, his feelings hidden.

"What, do you two have something going on?"

So much for keeping feelings hidden; he'd obviously failed in his attempt. "Not at all. I just wondered if she'd been by here when I was elsewhere. That's all."

"Well, she's kind of rough around the edges," Richard continued, totally unaware of how close he was to getting punched in the face. "But I could tame her, and have a good time doing it, too."

Warren barely kept from grinding his teeth with the effort it took to remain silent. Richard had always been quite the ladies' man. During the summers of his high school years, there wasn't a girl who would have turned down a date, and few who Richard didn't ask out at one time or other. It was a wonder he didn't have children from Oregon to Maine but as far as Warren knew, Richard just had one child, a daughter, back in New Orleans.

"How's Chloe?" he asked. If they were going to talk about females, Warren much preferred to switch the topic to one who was a child.

"She's a sweetheart," Richard replied, instantly smiling at the mention of his little girl. "Growing up too fast. Smart as a whip."

"Do you see her often?"

"Not as much as I'd like. Her mother is always tripping about child support, and uses the child as a bargaining chip."

Again, Warren had to bite his tongue. Some of the little girl's child support might have been spent on that premium leather upholstery in the car that he was now leaning against.

"I pay it, you know."

"Pay what?"

"Child support. Even give her more than is required by the courts. It's not the money Chloe's mother wants. It's me."

Warren felt bad about his assumption and vowed to be less judgmental about his friend. After all, there was a good side to Richard, the side that his child's mother probably wanted back in her life. He looked at his watch and pushed off. "I'm going to get out of here. If you don't have plans tonight, you're welcome to my parents for their nightly roundtable, otherwise known as the evening meal."

"Thanks, man, but I think I'm going to hit this club I heard about, the new one just outside Paradise Cove."

"The Groove?"

"Yes, that's it. Met a woman the other night who told me their happy hours are pretty good."

"All right, then, Rich. I'll see you sometime next week."

"Not on Monday?"

"No. Now that the harvest is underway and Jackson's men have the house building under control, I'll more than likely spend most of next week at the realty office."

"Hey, where exactly does your neighbor live? I might need to check in on her next week, see if she needs any help with anything."

"She more than likely should run away from any type of help you're offering," Warren said, a smile and light tone belying the seriousness of his statement. "You're here to work, not chase skirts."

"A brother like me has to do both," Richard countered, opening his car door to get in. "But no worries. You know the deal. You're talking to Richard Cunningham. The cunning man. There's never been a woman that I've set in my sights and then not spent the night!"

"On that note…" Warren shook his head and got into his newly purchased SUV, the other piece of business that he'd handled this week after deciding against using his sports car to do regular jaunts in this bumpy terrain.

The men waved as they each took off down the gravel drive, one that would be smooth concrete once finished. Warren tried not to think about them, but Richard's parting words continued to play in his head. It shouldn't have come as a surprise that Richard was interested in Charli. After all, she was female and breathing. And he didn't even try and figure out why the thought bothered him so. He just knew that it did.

Before Warren reached Paradise Cove's city limits, he knew something else. For his playboy friend Richard to get to Charli, he'd have to come through him.

Chapter 13

Charli didn't head straight home after her encounter with Warren. With her feelings roiling and her body still reeling from his touch, she headed for the open prairie, where both her horse and her thoughts could run wild. She knew Griff was waiting on her, that supper was probably ready. But she also knew that in the presence of the man who'd known her since she wore pigtails and patent leather she wouldn't be able to hide the fact that she was flummoxed. And that was putting it mildly.

She reached the far end of her property and dismounted, leaving Butterscotch to munch on grass and daisies. She meandered toward a copse of trees, her hands in her back pockets, trying to figure out how to reconcile her opposing thoughts. She shouldn't like Warren. He was a Drake. Her grandfather had never had anything good to say about them. Had said that they were condescending and highfalutin. *Bourgie* was another description he'd use, his mouth often twisted in a scowl as he said it. Once, when she had asked why he didn't like them, he'd responded, *Because they don't think their feces has an odor.* Except he'd used other, more direct yet equally descriptive words. She'd worshipped the ground that Charles Reed walked on. So if he hadn't liked them, how could she? Yet how could she deny the feelings that were evoked just now when Warren had held her? In his arms, she'd experienced a feeling that she'd never felt before. Not even with her ex-fiancé. Not with her first crush back in high school. Not with anyone.

Looking up, she noticed the sun sinking. It was time to head home. Her cell phone was in her saddlebag. Undoubtedly it held a missed call and perhaps a message from Griff, inquiring as to her whereabouts. Sometimes she teased that he was worse than a mother hen when it came to her safety. She couldn't imagine life without him.

Retrieving her phone, she touched the screen to light it up. There had been one missed call. She read the number and frowned. Not one that she recognized. But since it wasn't unusual for someone to call her cell instead of the office phone with dairy questions, she immediately hit redial—and regretted it as soon as she heard the voice on the other end.

"Cedric? How did you get my number?" she seethed as he shared how he'd lied to Alice. "If you call again, I'm going to report it as harassment. Got it?" The sound of his voice offering an explanation grated on her ears and made her hands shake. She ended the call while he was in midsentence, threw the phone into her bag and rode away.

Moments later she reached her ranch house. That it needed a fresh coat of paint did not go without notice. But the hydrangeas were flourishing and the beauty of those bushes alone, with their blue, pink, white and purple flowers, covered a multitude of faults.

"About time," Griff grunted as soon as she walked in the door.

"Something smells good," Charli responded.

"Something called supper. Which you missed. Some of the guys wanted to wait but couldn't. They had chores."

"Sorry!" she yelled from the kitchen.

Minutes later, she walked into the living/dining area and sat at the table. Smells from the plate of piping-hot chicken-fried steak, mashed potatoes, green beans and sliced onions, all from their land, tickled her olfactory senses and made her stomach growl. She dug in.

Griff got up from his well-worn recliner, passed her and walked into the kitchen. He returned moments later with a large glass of lemonade and a saucer of rolls, which he set in front of her.

"Thanks," she mumbled around a mouthful of food.

He walked back into the kitchen, returned to the dining room with a slice of homemade apple pie and sat at the table.

"This is good, Griff," she said, pausing to wipe her mouth and have a drink of lemonade.

Griff grunted.

"Did Bobby tell you about the cow?"

He nodded. "More meat for winter."

"Hated to lose it, though. Was hoping we might get another calf out of her, or two."

"We could have used 'em. Going to have to sell another chunk of the stock as it is."

Charli set down her fork. "Why?"

Griff took his time cutting off a bite of pie and eating it. "Water tank's leaking. And we need to put a patch on the roof. Heard birds or rats or something flitting around."

"Oh, man."

The sketchy economy in the last few years had not been kind to dairy farmers, which was one of the reasons Charli had moved back from Oakland. Her grandfather had worked hard for this farm and on this land. And while she'd received a good many offers to buy her out, she was determined not to sell.

"I'd rather not lose any more livestock, especially heifers. What about a loan?"

"Don't like owing nobody. Charles didn't, either."

"Well, he isn't here. And I'm determined to keep up our head count. So give me a couple days to try and figure something out."

"Don't worry about it, Charli. We'll be okay."

"I know we will, Griff." She placed her hand over his and felt her throat constrict. With her mother remarried and living in Canada, Griff was the closest thing to a relative that she had in the West. "Somehow, we always manage."

They continued to eat, mostly in silence. When they talked, it was on lighter topics: the weather, baseball—Griff's favorite sport—and current news. They didn't return to the subject of money or the ranch. But for the rest of the evening, this very real dilemma was very much on her mind.

Money, or specifically the lack of it, was not a concern for anyone living within the guarded, gated community rather appropriately called Golden Gates. This fact was no more evident than in the Drake household as members of Ike and Jennifer's family sat around the table feasting on Russian osetra caviar and toast points and drinking pricey champagne. A rack of lamb was warming in the oven and would be accompanied by organic root vegetables and a spicy couscous. This balmy Friday evening saw some of their children enjoying plans of their own, dates and the like, but four of the eight in their brood—Niko, Warren and the twins, Terrell and Teresa—joined Ike and Jennifer at the table.

"I hear you had a run-in with your neighbor," Niko said,

pouring more champagne into his flute. "You know we've got a history with the Reeds."

Warren gave his parents a look before responding. He did this even though he knew that with few secrets within this close-knit clan, having his siblings all up in his business was to be expected.

"I do now. And I wouldn't call it a run-in. It was more like a misunderstanding."

"She sure did grow into a beautiful woman," Niko continued after enjoying a bite of caviar. "I hadn't seen her in years, almost didn't recognize her when I saw her at the dance."

"She was there?" Terrell asked. "What does she look like?"

Warren would have supplied this information except Niko beat him to it. "She was the tall sister in that strapless, slinky dress, with those well-defined arm muscles and legs for days."

"The one that you were dancing with, Warren?" Teresa asked. Warren nodded.

"Damn, she is fine!" Terrell exclaimed. Jennifer's brow raised. "I mean, darn. Sorry, Mom."

"Yes," she teased. "I just bet you are."

"How's your house coming along?" Teresa asked.

"Jackson thinks it will be finished ahead of schedule. And thanks to Dexter, the harvest is right on schedule as well. So far so good with everything I've planned."

Except my progress on a friendship with Charli.

Ike sat back, watching as the housekeeper came in and removed their appetizer dishes. "Jackson still here?"

Warren shook his head. "He's left the work in the capable hands of his foreman for this region, a nice family man named Brandon. He said he'll more than likely be back next week, once they get ready to install the pool."

"It sounds as though your home will be lovely, dear.

Would you like my assistance in planning the housewarming?"

"I don't know, Mom. Hadn't even thought about having a party."

"That's what moms are for, my sweet, to think of these things for you. Until you get a wife, that is. And then she'll do it."

Warren almost spewed his bubbly. "Wife! Where'd that come from?"

"Don't say the word like it's poison, son," Ike said, his voice filled with humor. "Eight kids and only one of y'all married. You'll be thirty years old next year. It's time to start thinking about your legacy."

"I'll think about mine after Niko thinks about his."

"Don't pull me into it," Niko said, smiling at the housekeeper as she sat down a silver tray holding the rack of lamb and vegetables. He reached for the serving spoon and passed it to his mom. "I'm going to be a bachelor for life!"

"Me, too," Warren added.

"That's what we all say," Ike commented, lifting his plate to receive a serving of lamb. "Usually right before we find the one that makes us want to marry!"

As soon as he said this, an image flashed in Warren's mind: of dusty jeans and sweat-stained tees, a straw cowboy hat and scruffy boots. It made no sense, but the more he thought about it, he couldn't help but wonder if just such a woman for him might be as close as his next-door neighbor.

Chapter 14

It had been an exceptional week at the office and by Thursday, when Warren took a break to check out the progress on his new home, he was in a cheerful mood. Even as the housing market continued to waver in light of the nation's economy, the family business, Drake Realty Plus, had shown steady profits for the past six months.

Most of this was due to the Paradise Cove expansion and the condominium complex that had been built on the town's north side. That and the newest subdivision, Seventh Heaven, with large, energy-efficient homes competitively priced and built almost exclusively by Warren's cousin-in-law Jackson's company, Boss Construction. The subdivision was nearly sixty percent sold, with most being purchased from the blueprints stage. And finally, he would see the first yield from his grape crop divided up and sold to a jelly and jam processing company and a grape juice manufacturer, with the balance sent to Dexter for another brand of Drake wine. Yes, the Drakes had a lot to be thankful for. This was going to be another stellar year.

Just as he was about to turn off onto the two-lane highway leading to his ranch he saw a sign: Cows for Sale. *Charli.* He bypassed his turn and continued on down the road, following the crudely drawn arrow underneath the words. About a mile down the road was another sign, about thirty yards from a tarred driveway, announcing this as the place to buy prime beef.

Warren turned into the drive and stopped in front of a white rambling farmhouse with black stucco trim. Just beyond it was a red gambrel-roofed barn with stark white trim that looked straight out of an episode of *Little House on the Prairie.* He exited his car, walked up to the wide, wraparound porch and knocked on the door.

Within a half an hour he'd made his purchase, arranged for delivery and continued down the road. When he passed Charli's ranch he smiled, imagining the look on her face when the farmer showed up on her doorstep with his purchase. A superior breed, according to the seller, with a long German-sounding name and a pedigree that the farmer swore went back to the year 1541.

Well...all righty then. Warren had to take the man's word for it. The most he knew about those four-legged creatures was the type of cut he preferred on his plate.

Charli had just returned from a run to the feed store when she saw the black pickup with high side rails ambling down their long driveway. *That looks like the Dohertys' truck. Wonder what they want.* She quickly went through their inventory in her head, trying to remember if a bill for any of their livestock had gone unpaid. She stood by her truck until they'd parked, then walked over as old man Doherty and a young man who Charli guessed might be his grandson got out of the truck.

"Afternoon, Charli!"

"Afternoon, Mr. Doherty. What can I do for you?" She looked at the little boy, smiled and nodded and could now see the head of a cow through the rails.

"This is my grandson, Harry. Harry, say hello to Ms. Reed."

"Hi, ma'am."

"Hi, Harry." She looked back at Mr. Doherty. "What brings you out our way?"

Mr. Doherty motioned her to follow him. "Brought you something," he threw over his shoulder.

Charli fell in step behind him, her brow furrowed in curiosity. Once she saw what was in the back of his truck, her curiosity turned to confusion. "A heifer and a steer," she said, reaching her hand between the rails to pet one of them. "Vorderwalds, right?"

"You got it."

She whistled. "I know they're worth every penny, but they're too rich for my blood." She walked around the truck, inspecting the beef, trying to figure out how she could buy when her somewhat precarious financial situation said that they needed to sell. "How much are you asking for them? Wait, let me rephrase that. How much are you asking for one? I could really use that heifer."

Mr. Doherty had gone around to the back of the truck, raised the slide on the railing and unhooked the gate. "Won't cost you nothing." He looked up as Griff came out on the porch. "Hey there, partner."

"Hey, Joe." Griff continued down the steps and joined them at the back of the truck. "You're doing door-to-door cow selling these days?"

"No," Mr. Doherty said with a chuckle. "Came to drop these off."

Both Griff and Charli's heads shot up.

"What do you mean?" Charli asked.

Griff simply stared.

"Wait, you must have heard that I had to put a cow down last week. But how?"

"Harry, get up there and rope 'em up. Then pull down the ramp so we can walk 'em off of it."

"No, wait, Harry." Charli looked at Mr. Doherty. "I appreciate you coming over, but we can't afford these."

"Don't have to. They're paid for."

"What? Who? How?" Now Charli was totally flustered.

"Your neighbor, Warren Drake."

Charli's jaw dropped.

"He said he saw my sign and came over. Of course, he'd planned to buy only one, but you know what a salesman I am." Mr. Doherty's blue eyes sparkled. "I made him an offer that he couldn't refuse.

"Didn't I, Harry?"

"Yessir!"

Charli was stunned. She knew her mouth should be moving but couldn't think of one thing to say.

Griff could. And did. "Tell you what. You take those cows right on down the road to his place."

"What?" Charli's voice was incredulous. She hadn't even had to think; the word seemed to come out of its own volition.

"We don't need charity." He shot a stream of tobacco at a vibrant blue, perfectly formed hydrangea. *Bull's-eye.* "And we don't need to be in debt to a Drake."

"But, Griff—"

"No buts."

Charli looked at Mr. Doherty. "Excuse us a minute." She took Griff's arm and pulled him several yards away from where the Dohertys were standing. "What are you doing?"

Griff's eyes narrowed. "A better question is what is he doing?"

"Perhaps he's just trying to be a good neighbor. He was there when I had to put her down."

Griff spat again.

"We didn't ask him to buy the cattle." Silence. "Griff, this is a blessing, an answer to a prayer that I didn't even send up!"

If there was a way for silence to deepen, Griff had found it.

"Aren't you the one who taught me not to look a gift horse in the mouth?"

Griff shifted from one foot to the other. "I also taught you that nothing in life is free."

"Fine. I'll talk to him, set up some kind of payment arrangement."

"Have you considered that money may not be the means of exchange he has in mind?"

The question gave her pause. "What are you saying?"

Silence once again. But no matter. The look that he gave her spoke volumes.

"We're keeping those cattle, Griff. Whatever the payment, we'll work it out."

"You take those cows and your grandfather is liable to not only turn over in his grave, but to jump up out of it."

"Well, if he does," Charli said after a long pause, "then *he* can take the cows to Drake!"

Chapter 15

Charli swore that the only reason she'd changed into her nice jeans and pink ruffled top was because of the shift in the weather, and that she wore gloss because her lips were dry. Her hair, well, a girl had to wash it sometimes, right? It hung wild and loose, the curls swinging around her face as she bounced down the road in her trusty pickup, and after much argument and cajoling, one of Griff's freshly made apple pies sat in the passenger seat.

She turned into the Drake driveway and saw a flurry of activity happening up ahead. Her stomach fluttered. *Maybe I should have called.* But at the exact moment she thought to turn around, Warren looked up. And waved. No way to back out now. She parked next to a shiny new SUV, reached for the pie and jumped down from the cab before nonstop thoughts made her lose her nerve. Before she cleared her truck bed, Warren had broken away from the group of men and was walking her way.

"Hello."

It was just a word, but the way he delivered it made her want to see the eyes hidden behind dark shades. He looked manly and rugged, adapting to the countryside in his beat-up jeans and cowboy boots. Who was this buckaroo, and what happened to the tux-wearing, diamond stud-sporting Fred Astaire she'd danced with two weeks ago?

"Thank you."

Warren removed his glasses, looked down at the box she held and then back at her. "You're welcome."

"This is for you." Charli held out the pie box and cursed herself for the breathy way she was talking, the way her hands were shaking, and the way her heart was getting ready to beat right out of her chest.

He took the box. Their fingers touched. Sparks flew. Muscles clenched in hidden places.

"Did you make this?" he asked, raising the lid and sniffing the contents.

"No. Griff is the main cook in the house. But I can hold my own," she added, lest he think that she couldn't boil an egg.

"It smells delicious."

"It is." A brief, awkward silence and then, "Why'd you do it?"

"Buy the cows?" He shrugged. "You lost one. I saw the sign." She frowned. "It's Thursday and I'm in a good mood. Heck, I don't know! I didn't think about it. I just did it."

"I can't accept them as a gift, you know."

Warren's expression changed from one of relaxed camaraderie to mild frustration. "No, I don't know."

Charli swallowed, trying to find courage in the face of his stare. "If you'll just tell me how much you paid for them, I can set up a plan to pay you back."

Warren's eyes narrowed. "Does this have anything to do with the beef—no pun intended—that supposedly happened between our grandfathers? Because I can't think of any other reason that you'd act this ungrateful."

No, he didn't just talk to me like I was twelve. Anger flashed, hot and immediate. Charli was thankful. Anger was good. Anger would put her back in a place that was familiar and take her out of the murky emotional waters that she was now treading.

"How dare you! I am *not* ungrateful! I came over here to thank you, to show my appreciation, the expression of which you are now holding in your hands!"

"What I'm holding is a pie that somebody else made. So it would seem that Griff is thankful. Am I to assume that he speaks for you?"

How in the world was what she thought could be a potentially flirtatious occasion now going to hell in a handbasket?

She crossed her arms. "Griff warned me not to take them. He said that your motives would not be pure."

Warren took a step toward her. "Oh, he did, did he?"

Charli willed herself not to shrink back. Instead, she lifted her chin a notch. "Yes. He did."

Without another word, Warren spun around and stalked to the SUV that was parked beside her truck. He got in it, started it up and spewed gravel as he backed out and headed down the driveway.

It all happened so quickly that it took a moment for Charli's brain to communicate the obvious. *He's headed to my house!*

She ran to her pickup, jumped in the cab and started it up before her door was shut. Gravel flew again as she raced to catch up with the shiny new SUV, probably pulling with eight cylinders compared to her six. "Oh my God," she mumbled, shifting into fifth gear and willing her pickup to, well, pick up speed. "Please let Griff be gone to get groceries!"

Because she had a feeling if the two men met up before she reached them, it wouldn't be nice.

She turned off the end of the driveway, and the truck sputtered and died. She pressed on the gas pedal. Nothing.

"No!" She pumped the pedal and turned the key. Still, the truck refused to speak. The battery had been giving her hints, nudges, warnings that it needed to be replaced. Warnings that she should have heeded because now her truck battery was dead.

Hopefully, no human she knew would share this fate.

Warren reached the Reed property and took the turn on two wheels. He hadn't been this angry since…well…in a long darn time! The nerve of someone to call his character into question. To assume that his random act of kindness had strings attached. To suggest that being kin to Walter Drake was akin to being shady. Walter Drake was a stalwart, upright man. Griff or any other dirt dabbler could only wish he could measure up to the heels on his grandfather's wing-tipped shoes!

He reached the house and brought his SUV to a screeching halt in the middle of the driveway. He was breathing heavy and his heart raced; he was so angry that he even scared himself. *Man, you've got to calm down!* Still, he flexed his hands and balled them into fists, taking a moment to relish the idea of one of them connecting to the mouth that talked trash against him.

"No, you're not going to get physical," he mumbled aloud, working to calm his irate nerves. "You're better than that. You're a man. And you're getting ready to show this old-school fool what one looks like."

He opened the car door, calmly walked up on the Reed porch, crossed to the heavy wooden front door and knocked.

Once.

Twice.

No answer.

He looked around and noted several cars about, including an old Ford pickup that looked a lot like Griff, whether it belonged to the old geezer or not.

He turned back to the door. And knocked harder. *Bang!*

The door opened with a jerk.

Griff was chewing his ever-present toothpick. His face was set. His eyes were narrowed. "What the hell you want?"

Warren took a breath. "My grandfather, Walter Drake, taught me to respect my elders. So, *Mr.* Griff, I want to know what I ever did to you to cause you to take my name and drag it through the Reed land mud?"

Chapter 16

Griff eyed the young upstart trying to hold onto his temper. He looked beyond him for Charli's truck. Didn't see it. But something told him that the fact that Warren was standing before him had everything to do with Charli's visit to his ranch. And something told him it wasn't about whether there'd been too much cinnamon in the pie.

"Where's Charli?"

Warren looked behind him and then turned back to Griff. "I don't know. But she's not who I've come to visit. I've come to see you, Mr. Griff. To talk man to man. Because somewhere along the way you've gotten the mistaken notion that you know me. I'm here to clear up some areas where you've clearly gotten it wrong."

After what seemed like a pause long enough to drive an omnibus through, Griff stepped out onto the porch. "I'm listening."

"First of all, I'm not a shady person, nor do I execute business deals in an underhanded way. If I were looking for something, payment of some kind, for the cows I purchased, I would have negotiated the fee up front.

"Secondly, there was absolutely no forethought put into my buying the cows for Charli. *Charli,* Mr. Griff, not you. It happened on the spur of the moment, after my company had experienced a relatively good week. I was in a good mood and wanted to do something nice for someone who I felt deserved it. Period. End of story.

"Thirdly, and finally, I don't buy women, and I damn sure don't buy them with cows!"

Warren's chest heaved with the force of his passion. Griff calmly cleaned his fingernails with the toothpick he'd pulled from his mouth.

"Well?" Warren said at last. "Are you going to deny that you said I had ulterior motives? Do you have anything at all to say to me?"

"Maybe," Griff drawled, after another moment had passed. "But it might go down better with a taste." He turned, walked toward the front door and said with his back to Warren's scowl, "Come on in."

With only a slight hesitation, Warren followed Griff into the house. He took in the cozy, lived-in atmosphere at once: dark wood floors, a long, leather couch, a well-worn recliner, two rocking chairs, a cowhide rug, afghan throws and a huge, rugged dining room table that looked as though it had been built on site from some of the oak trees out back. The boards were held together with huge iron studs and the top appeared to be at least six inches thick. A few items that signaled a woman's touch kept the dark room from being too manly: gingham curtains, gilt-framed pictures and a vase of flowers sitting atop the table, hydrangeas that had obviously been picked from the outside bushes.

Griff turned, holding two bottles. "This here weak stuff or my homemade hooch?"

Warren eyed the bottle of store-bought scotch in Griff's left hand and the unlabeled bottle containing clear liquid in his right. This was a test, he knew. Warren determined that he would pass it if it killed him. He might not have been so gung ho if he'd known it likely could. "I'll have what you're having."

An eyebrow shot up. "You sure about that?"

"What doesn't kill me will make me stronger, right?"

Griff pulled two shot glasses from off the hutch and filled them with the clear liquid. Warren walked over to where he stood as Griff held up a glass. Warren took it, braced himself and after Griff had lifted his glass in a silent toast, slammed it back.

And like to have died.

To say that the liquid burned going down was an understatement. No, it felt as if someone had taken a lit torch and stuck it down his throat *after* it had been coated with butane. But he took it like a man, refusing to gasp or drop to his knees the way he wanted to do. He felt sweat pop out on his brow and under his arms. Still, he'd swallowed the conflagration masquerading as alcohol and—aside from his eyes watering and a lone tear escaping from the side of his left one, one he surreptitiously swiped away—had shown no outer reaction.

Griff, who'd downed the drink like water, simply licked his lips.

Warren figured that Griff was waiting for him to say something. *Wonder if you can talk without a voice box?* He seriously questioned whether or not he had one left.

The merest upturning of Griff's mouth before he held up the bottle. "Another?"

Warren gave one single head shake, even as he tested his tongue to see if it could move.

"Sure?"

He swallowed again. *Okay, maybe there's hope that I*

can still talk. "That's…" He stopped, cleared his throat and tried to bring it back to its normal register instead of the pitch about an octave above it that he'd just heard. "That's good stuff."

Griff knocked back the second shot and placed the glass on the table. Warren finished another shot and set down his glass, too. Thankfully.

"Have a seat," Griff said, walking over to the recliner.

After taking a tentative step to make sure his leg didn't wobble, Warren followed him into the living room, taking a seat on the well-worn brown couch. He wasn't much of a drinker. Which might explain why after two shots of Griff's brew he felt he needed coffee, or sleep.

"What was that?" he asked.

"The drink?"

Warren nodded.

"Corn liquor, my special brew." Griff smiled, revealing a row of white teeth interrupted by a gold one on the side. "It'll put hair on your chest."

"If that's the case, I probably could pass for an ape right about now."

"Ha!" Griff reached for a tobacco pouch on the table beside him, turned it back and forth in his hand. "Most folk can't handle the first sip. They either spit or gag." He gave Warren a look that came precariously close to respectful.

Quiet ensued. Warren again looked around the room where Charli spent time, where he imagined she'd grown up. But had she? He wasn't sure and in this moment realized just how little he knew about his neighbor. Then, remembering Griff's reaction the last time she was mentioned, he decided on a different line of conversation.

"What happened between Mr. Reed and my grandfather?"

Griff's mouth set into a hard line. He looked away from

Warren, out the plate-glass window into the expansive backyard. "Walter still living?"

"Yes."

"Ask him."

"That's fair." More silence and then Warren bit the bullet—talking about the person who was really on his mind. "I mean no harm to Charli."

The pause was so long that Warren wondered whether Griff had heard, or if he'd answer. But he finally did. "Time will tell."

"Yes, it will. And I hope that when time proves that I'm a gentleman, you'll be around to see it."

"Oh, I'll be here," Griff said, his eyes narrowing as he fixed an unflinching gaze on Warren. "It was Charles's dying request for me to look after her. I gave him my word. My word is my bond."

"So is mine." Warren's gaze was unwavering as well.

"Fair enough." Griff stood. "Another shot?"

Warren reared back against the couch and crossed his right ankle over his left knee. He knew that later he would pay for it, knew that there was a good chance that after today he'd never be able to taste anything for the rest of his life. Not with fried taste buds. But he knew what Griff was doing and was determined to match him round for round. That's why as much as he still felt his insides rumbling from the last one, he gave a slow smile and answered, "Sure."

Chapter 17

Blasted bum battery! Charli thanked the man who'd helped her push her truck back from the two-lane road before he used his cables to jump it. She barely allowed him time to get the hood closed before she put the jalopy into gear and was flying back down the street. Gravel flew everywhere as she turned onto the paved lane, racing the short distance to Reed Ranch. Various scenarios and images played in her head, none of them good. With two men as proud and stubborn as Griff and Warren, she had no doubt that she'd arrive to spilled blood. The only question in her mind was which one would get the worst of the fight. Warren was younger but when it came to stamina and determination, Griff took that hands down.

She sped up, pushed the old Ford to its limit. When she reached the turn into the Reed Ranch drive, she banged her hand against the wheel as a tractor pulling a thirty-foot bed of steel pipes, going all of thirty-five miles an hour, chose this exact time to pass her driveway. As soon as she could get around it she turned left, half of the truck on pavement and half on grass. Her heart skittered around inside her chest like a Ping-Pong ball.

The front yard came into view. She looked for bodies. No one was sprawled on the grass. To the right was Griff's pickup and beside it Warren's SUV. Her brow creased. *Where are they? The house?* Overturned furniture and broken glass immediately came to mind. She threw the truck into Park, stomped on the emergency brake and jumped out almost before the wheels stopped rolling.

Rushing up the steps, she heard something that stopped her in her tracks: laughter.

What? She turned and looked again. Maybe she'd just imagined that Warren's SUV was still parked on the property. Nope. It was definitely there. She couldn't recall hearing Warren laugh but that low, raspy chuckle coming through the screen door was definitely Griff. She took a breath, squared her shoulders and marched inside.

"Charli!" Griff's voice was animated and his eyes were bright. "Where you been, girl?"

Her eyes narrowed. There was only one thing that made Griff talk loud and act so jubilant: moonshine.

She looked at Warren. "Drake, what's going on here?"

Warren offered a lopsided smile. "Griff was sharing your Annie Oakley stories. How you killed a snake in the henhouse with one shot, then brought it out hanging over the gun."

"Remember that, Charli?" Griff asked, his voice filled with affection. "I think you were around ten years old."

Suddenly shy, Charli shifted from one foot to the other. "I don't think you'll ever let me forget."

"The gun was almost as tall as she was," Griff said to Warren, leaning toward him and talking in a conspiratorial tone as if they were best buds. "Charles was proud as a peacock. Called her a chip off the old block."

She smiled in spite of her trepidation at what other stories Griff had shared. There were one or two things in her childhood past that she wished to stay there. "That's a monster of a house you're building," she said to change the subject. "How many bedrooms is it?"

"Four bed, four and a half bath," Warren responded.

"Only four bedrooms? It looks bigger."

"Jackson, that's my contractor, has added a few bonus rooms—theater, solarium, butler's pantry—places I'll probably rarely visit. But he said it would be good for the resale value." He saw a look pass between Griff and Charli and realized that maybe he'd said too much. It was obvious from the looks of their home that for them money might be an issue. He was the last one who'd want to make them self-conscious about their lack of wealth.

Fortunately he was saved by the bell, otherwise known as the ringer on his cell phone. He reached for it and looked down. "Excuse me," he said before taking the call. "Hello?" He paused, watching as Charli walked to the hutch and poured a glass of water. Mindful that Griff was also watching, he made sure to keep his eyes above her waist. "No, I'm close. Right down the street." He stood. "No problem, I'm on my way. Be there in five minutes."

"That was my brother. He's down at the property. I need to meet him there." Walking over with hand outstretched he said, "Mr. Griff, thanks for the hospitality, and the drink."

"I'll walk you out."

"Charli, I'll see you later."

She made no move toward him, but her eyes were soft as she answered, "See you later, Drake."

The two men were silent as they walked toward Warren's car. When they reached it, Griff held out his hand. "Thanks for the cattle."

Warren shook it. "You're welcome."

"It's a big help."

Warren nodded. "I'm glad we had this time to talk, Mr. Griff."

"Just Griff is fine."

"Yes, sir." He opened his car door.

"Drake?"

"Yes, sir?"

"To answer your question, Griff is my first name."

Warren smiled. "Yes, sir. Bye, Griff."

He started his car, continuing to smile as he drove down their drive. He couldn't help but marvel at how different he felt going than he had coming. On the way there, he'd been madder than a hornet. Now he felt as if he'd made a new friend. He felt the beginning of a headache, too, and hoped someone at the site had aspirin. Griff's liquor had been lethal, but after drinking water for the last hour at least he was somewhat sober.

So yes, he felt he'd finally melted some of the ice around Griff's heart, and maybe Charli's, too. Griff's hooch, on the other hand, had melted Warren's insides. Risky move going toe to toe with a man as tough as the old ranch hand. Only time would tell if it had been worth it.

Chapter 18

Is that my place? Man, Jackson wasn't kidding when he said that they were going to use that crew to speed things up even more because another project fell through. Just five days ago, when Warren left the Reed Ranch and met his brother Niko at the site, the house had been almost a shell. Sure, concrete had been poured and a few walls were up. But this right here? This was…a house! He continued to marvel as he parked his SUV and got out.

He spotted Jackson immediately and walked over. "Hey, Boss. What did you guys do, work around the clock since I last saw this place?"

Jackson smiled. "Just about."

"I'm impressed."

"Keep being impressed when you get the bill for the overtime you approved."

"Overtime? What are you talking about?"

"Don't even try it. I gave you a projection of the added cost and asked for your approval. You signed it."

"Oh, man." Warren rubbed his head. "You took advantage!"

"How so?"

"You did that last week. I told you and Niko that I'd drank some of Griff's home brew."

"You didn't act drunk."

"That doesn't mean some of my brain cells hadn't dissolved!"

"Ha!"

"It's okay, man," Warren said, looking around. "This place looks great. So what's next?"

"The plumbing is completely done. We've almost got all of the electrical wiring in. If we stay on schedule, the company we've subcontracted to do your pool, spa and fountains will be here shortly to start that installation."

"I know that you normally leave jobs like these to your trusty foremen, but I appreciate you personally overseeing so much of my construction. The time away from your wife and family is a sacrifice. So thank you, man. For real."

"No worries, Warren. I like to get out of the office and get in the thick of construction on a regular basis. Keeps me sharp and on the cutting edge of new innovations."

"Well, whenever you and your family are in the area, know that you'll always have a place to stay."

Warren's phone rang. He didn't recognize the number but answered right away. "Hello?"

"Drake."

His heart palpitated as though he were a randy teen with a schoolboy crush. Still, when he spoke it was as though he was the maestro of cool. He gave Jackson a nod before walking away to take the call in private. "The name's Warren."

"Isn't it also Drake?"

"Sure, Reed," he answered with a smile in his voice. "But most people call me by my first name."

"I guess I'm not most people."

He allowed his voice to go low and velvety. "You're most certainly not."

A short pause. She cleared her throat.

Warren second-guessed his mack daddy move. True, they'd made progress. But the chances of this being a social call were still relatively slim. "Is everything all right?"

"Sure, everything's fine."

You sure are. Warren had the presence of mind not to voice this thought. "How's Griff?"

She laughed, a sound he hadn't heard before. He immediately knew that he wanted to hear a lot more of it.

"Whatever you did the other day impressed him. And that's rare."

"I drank fire."

Another chuckle. "He told me about that. Said that you tried not to react even though there were tears streaming down your face and smoke coming out your ears!"

"Only one tear. And no smoke."

"If you say so."

Warren walked over and leaned against his vehicle, trying to remember the last time simply talking to a person had made him feel this good.

"You're probably busy so—"

"No, I've got time."

"There's a reason why I called you."

"What's up?"

"It's about the cows you bought."

"Charli, let's not go there again."

"No, this isn't about paying for them or giving them back."

"Then what?"

"It's just that…"

He heard her sigh, and remembered the way her breath felt against his cheek that night when they were dancing.

And how her breasts had felt crushed against his chest that day by the fence. He wanted to feel more of her. Much more. Despite that it was the middle of the day and that he was a stone's throw from a group of sweaty men, his groin tightened. He began walking toward his office to… move things around.

"What is it, Charli?"

"We need to sell a cow. One of yours."

He stopped, and then continued walking. "Is that all?"

"Isn't that enough? It isn't easy to ask if something given as a gift can be turned around and sold for profit. But we've got a couple of emergencies. A leak in the water tank and a part of the roof that—"

"Charli, there's no need to explain. Once I gave you the cattle they were yours to do with as you wished."

"Maybe, but I didn't want my actions to appear ungrateful."

Her answer was soft and Warren imagined that almost smile that he'd come to expect, and to love.

"You didn't even have to tell me." Now his voice too was soft, and caring.

"Yes, I did."

They hung up shortly after that, both going on about their day. But for Warren, the sun seemed to shine just a little bit brighter, the grass seemed to be just a little greener and a place that was exclusively reserved for Charli opened up inside his heart.

The next morning, Warren was up and at his ranch bright and early. He had a meeting with the vineyard manager and planned to spend the morning learning more about grapes and the overall operation. He'd gotten a text from Jackson letting him know that the swimming pool crew had arrived and that excavation would begin shortly. Everything seemed to be humming along smoothly. His home would be finished ahead of schedule, the first vineyard yield was a bumper crop, he'd made peace with Griff and felt a closer bond with Charli. Only Tuesday and his week was off to a stellar start. How could it get any better?

He'd just turned on his iPod and was bobbing his head to the sounds of Prince's greatest hits when his phone rang. He tapped the speaker button. "Yes, Boss."

"Warren, we've just finished digging the hole for the pool. But I think you need to come over here before we go any further."

Warren detected a seriousness to Jackson's normally casual tone. He sat up straighter. "Okay. Is there a problem?"

"No, no problem. Uh, I just want you to check something out."

"Can it wait until later? After I finish reviewing these books?"

"Dexter told me that once upon a time, gold had been found on this property. Is that right?"

"Yes, that's right."

"I'm no expert, but the subcontractor just brought me something that looks like a nugget. So I think you'd better come right now."

Chapter 19

Warren was up in a flash, curious as to what they'd found. Not that he expected that what Jackson had was the real thing. Charles Reed and his grandfather had already been there, done that, and not found any more gold. Still, he grabbed his keys and his phone and within minutes was zipping toward the construction site in his personal golf cart. He parked on the dirt some feet beyond the gaping hole and tried to appear nonchalant as he walked toward Jackson and the man Warren assumed was the subcontractor.

"Good morning, Boss." He turned to the stranger and held out his hand. "Warren Drake."

"Tom Peterson."

"Good to meet you."

"Warren," Jackson began, "first of all you should know that I've known Tom for more than a decade and would trust him like he was my brother. So you can feel safe discussing this around him. He won't break a confidence."

Jackson nodded at Tom, who took up the story.

"I was operating the hydraulic excavator and when I pulled up the bucket and saw something flashing in the mound of dirt, I immediately thought gold. I don't even know why, because I've never seen raw gold before. But I gave my men a ten-minute break and then went to get Jackson. That's when he called you."

"Because he showed me this." Jackson opened his palm.

Warren's curiosity immediately turned to excitement. He knew it in an instant, without even touching the piece, without further examination. His grandfather had a jar of nuggets that he kept on his desk. Nuggets that Warren and his brothers used to play with as children. He'd probably never know how his grandfather missed it during his search years ago, but there was no doubt about what Jackson held—a piece of solid gold.

He reached for it, and with his back to anyone who might be watching, held it to the sun. "Yes, this is a nugget. No doubt about it."

"Do you think there could be more of it?" Jackson asked.

"Hard to say, but I don't want you guys to do anything else here until I find out. Tom, is there any way we can suspend this job for today and have your guys come back tomorrow?"

"They won't feel too good about missing a day's pay but yes, we can do that."

Jackson spoke up. "Tom, I'll give four hours' pay to the men who are already here."

"I appreciate that."

Warren pulled out his phone. "I need to make a couple calls and then I'll know where to go from here."

Just as he was about to dial, he heard crunching gravel and looked up to see Richard approaching. Intuition kicked in. Warren pocketed the nugget.

Richard adjusted his sunglasses as he approached. "Morning, fellas!"

"Morning, Richard." Warren gave Richard a fist bump. Jackson and Tom also responded to his greeting. "How's it going?"

"Good. Good. They're doing the electrical wiring in the house right now, which is above both my skill set and my pay grade. So I thought I'd come over here and see if I could help with the pool that I'll hopefully be spending a lot of time chilling in next summer!"

"Did you ask Brandon about what other work was needed over there?" Jackson asked.

"Couldn't find him," Richard easily replied. "That's why I came looking for you." He looked around. "Though now that I think about it, I just saw what looked like the whole crew leaving as I walked over. Is everything okay?"

"Equipment situation," Jackson quickly answered, hoping that the noncommittal statement would suffice. "We're having to rearrange some things, shift some jobs around. So I'm going to have to ask some of the men to take the day off, you included. I'm going to still provide four hours' pay for everyone who has shown up."

Richard looked at Warren, who spoke up right away. "Looks like today is going to be an easy one for you, since it's just now ten o'clock. You've been talking about wanting to try out the golf course. I can give security a call so they'll let you through the gate, and you can get in eighteen holes."

Richard's look was contemplative as he nodded. "I just might take you up on that. But tell you what, I have something else that I need to take care of. So let me get back to you."

"All right, man. No problem. Go on and handle your business. We'll see you tomorrow." Warren waited until Richard was out of earshot and then turned back to the men. "I'm going to make these calls from my office. Jackson, I'll keep you posted."

"Okay. Sounds good."

Warren jumped back into the golf cart and headed to the office, but by the time he'd reached the vehicle-filled driveway, he'd changed his mind. This was a conversation with his father that he'd rather have face-to-face. He headed for his SUV and pulled out his phone.

"Hey, Dad," he said as soon as Ike answered. "Where are you? I'd like to come over for a minute." He got into his car and turned on the engine. "Why do I need to see you? What would you say if I told you that we've been excavating dirt to install the swimming pool…and found gold?"

Chapter 20

Warren drove through the towering, gold-plated gates that served as the entrance to a true paradise, the exlcusive Golden Gates enclave. Even though he'd been here practically his whole life, he still marveled at its opulence and beauty, still appreciated the grandiose entrance with its tons of flowers and spouting fountains and beyond it, the stately mansions and immaculately landscaped lawns. He went down the street and turned the corner into a cul-de-sac sporting only three homes: those of his oldest brother, Ike Jr.; his godparents, the Madisons; and his parents.

"Hello!" he announced, walking in the unlocked door. "Dad?"

"Back here, son."

Warren walked toward the back of the house and entered his father's home office/library. The faint smell of rich Dominican tobacco from Ike Sr.'s beloved Montecristo cigars tickled his nostrils as the blues music that often played low in the background of any room his father inhabited reached his ears.

He entered the room, his head immediately bobbing to the strains of B.B. King's guitar. "Hello, Dad."

Ike Sr. turned down the music. "Son!" He got up. They hugged. "Now, what in the world is this about finding gold?"

Warren reached into his pocket, pulled out the small nugget and set it on the shiny mahogany desktop.

Ike Sr. whistled as he sat back down. He picked up the nugget, turned and held it to the sunlight streaming in from the window behind him. "Well, there's no doubt. This is gold, all right. Daddy said there's no way that could happen. You know I called him as soon as we hung up the phone."

"I figured as much."

"Yes, he said that he and Charles spent almost three years, off and on, looking for more rocks. Said they'd dug up a good many acres trying to strike it rich, though he had to admit they didn't check all one thousand of them."

"Exactly."

Ike leaned forward, placed the phone on speaker and hit Redial. Soon the deep voice of his father, Walter Drake, filled the room. "I still don't believe it," he declared by way of greeting. "You rascals are trying to pull my leg."

"Believe it, Grandpa," Warren said, followed by a laugh.

"I'm looking at it right now, Daddy. It's sure enough gold."

"Well, I'll be damned. Where did you find it?"

Warren explained where on the ranch he'd planted the vineyards, and where in relation to those he was building his home and the swimming pool, where the nugget had been found.

"So you're talking about the southeast portion of the

property, right?" Walter asked. "Over there, close to the Reed property line."

"Not the furthermost part," Warren corrected. "And not necessarily so close to their line, either. I made sure to keep a good deal of land between my personal property and the fence. So if there's gold to be found, chances are it is now all on Drake property."

"Well, I'll be damned," Walter repeated, his voice a mixture of incredulity and respect. "Congratulations, boy. If you've indeed found gold, you've done what your grandfather tried to do and couldn't. Not after that little bit of luck we had just after we moved there. And that wasn't enough to retire on or anything, just enough to make us hungry enough to spend twice as much as what we'd found to try and locate more!"

The men laughed.

"I didn't know what to do next, Grandpa. That's why I'm calling."

"Well now, lookie here. I'm going to tell you exactly what you need to do."

Warren sat down and leaned forward, the second and third generation ready to listen to what the first generation had to say.

Someone else was listening, but no one was talking. Richard sat outside Acquired Taste, Paradise Cove's upscale restaurant and lounge located in a quaint strip mall about midway between Warren's ranch and the gated community of Golden Gates. He lounged in his Eldorado, nodding his head to his beloved old-school soul while listening even more closely to the intuition that had served him from the time he was the little boy of a single mother down in New Orleans, during his precarious years as a teen and young adult navigating the drug game and through four hard years in a federal prison. And his intuition was screaming that Warren was hiding something, that there was a reason that he'd wanted all the men gone from his place. But what?

That was the million-dollar question. Because for a man who had for the last three months said that moving into his ranch house was his top priority, Warren seemed a little too unconcerned today that work got done.

What's up with that?

Richard didn't know, but he planned to keep his eyes open—on the job site and off—to find out just why his inner voice was suggesting he pay attention.

He'd just changed the song on his stereo, going from the "Joy and Pain" of Frankie Beverly and Maze to the rich tenor voice of Eddie Kendricks when he saw her: medium height, long black hair, curves in all the right places. She was smartly dressed in a cute beige suit and high heels. Her sunglasses looked designer and her Louis Vuitton looked genuine. Richard had been sitting in his car trying to decide whether or not he wanted to eat in the restaurant or actually take Warren's advice and hit a drive-through before hitting the greens.

His decision had just been made. Totally confident in his looks, even in jeans and tee, he spritzed on a touch of designer cologne before exiting his car and strolling toward the restaurant entrance. Once inside, he squinted while his eyes adjusted to the darker interior. Looking for her.

"Good afternoon, sir," the cute brunette said to him, her bright smile rewarded with a smile of his own. "Welcome to Acquired Taste. Table for one?"

He found her. "I think I'll sit at the bar."

"Great idea. Enjoy!"

Richard strolled over and without looking at the woman, sat several stools away. It was a little early for the lunch crowd, so there was no one between them. He reached for the menu, placed a drink and food order and then busied himself checking messages and responding to Facebook posts on his cell phone.

Several moments passed. He received his brewski, took a swig...and waited.

"Excuse me."

Bingo! You've still got it, brother...you've still got it! But he ignored her. With a woman this beautiful, he knew that not being paid attention was rare.

"Excuse me," she said again, a little louder this time.

He liked the sound of her voice, light and cultured, strong enough to suggest that she wasn't a total pushover but light enough to tell him who'd be in control. He finally looked up. "Oh, sorry. I didn't know that you were talking to me."

"No problem."

She smiled. He liked that, too. Something about her seemed familiar. He rarely if ever forgot a pretty face. Then he remembered. He'd seen her the other night at the dance. If memory served him correctly, she'd talked to Warren at some point that night. *Interesting.* And perhaps advantageous. He turned on the charm, returning her smile while letting his bedroom eyes narrow ever so slightly, knowing that his long eyelashes now partly shielded his smoky orbs: a look that he knew drove women wild. Or so he'd been told.

She sat straighter in the bar seat. "I was just wondering if you were getting a signal in here. I've been trying to access the internet but it's not working."

"I'm on Facebook right now," he said, turning the face of his phone toward her so that she could see. "It's working for me just fine."

"You must have the touch," she responded. An obvious flirt.

"Indeed, I do," he said matter-of-factly, because it was the truth.

"Do you mind if I come over there? Maybe the internet just doesn't work on this side."

"It's a free country." This he said nonchalantly, as if he was too occupied to really care one way or another.

She picked up her glass of orange juice and moved to the chair next to his. "Hi. I'm Rachel."

"Richard," he said, still typing on his phone.

"I'm sorry for bothering you." She spoke with just the right amount of petulance in her voice to let Richard know that his ploy was working.

He finished the Facebook entry he was making, then lifted his head and looked at her. "Please accept my apologies," he murmured, seductive bass mixed with contriteness in his voice. "I didn't mean to ignore you. It's just that I've just reconnected with an old friend on Facebook, and was responding to an instant message that he'd sent."

Partly true. It was an old friend. Except *he* was female.

"Oh, it's okay. I just realized that you may be on the clock, or married, or simply not open to talking to strangers."

Nice try to find out if I'm available. I might be. But I'll keep you guessing. "I'm Richard Cunningham," he said, extending his hand.

"Nice to meet you, Richard."

He let his hand hold hers just a second longer than necessary before ending the handshake, then ran a finger over the softness of her palm. "You look familiar. Didn't I see you at the dance the other night?"

"The Days of Paradise Ball? Of course you saw me. I think everyone in town was there."

"Perhaps, but I don't remember everyone. Most of them didn't look as good as you."

She flushed, a pretty shade of pink on her bronzed skin. "Thank you."

"So, radiant Rachel, did you grow up here or are you a transplant like me?"

"I was born and raised in the Cove, left only briefly to attend college. I just graduated and have moved back until I figure out what's next in my life."

"This is a beautiful part of the country. It must have been nice growing up here."

"It definitely has its pluses. But there are minuses, too. The small-town mentality," she added when he raised a questioning brow. "Everybody knows your business, or thinks they do."

"I'm here helping out a friend of mine with a construction project. Warren Drake. Do you know him?"

It was brief, but Richard was nothing if not astute. He saw the flash of hurt in her eyes before she blinked it away, and immediately knew that this person might be useful for whatever might happen in the future.

"Yes, my older sister went to high school with Warren and our families travel in the same circle. How do you know him if you didn't grow up here?"

"I spent a lot of time at his grandfather's house in New Orleans. His grandmother and my mother became friends. When Warren came and stayed during the summer, we were almost inseparable. We attended the same college, too. After that we lost contact for a minute. But I'm glad we've reconnected. He's good people."

She didn't respond.

"So, Rachel…do you know any juicy gossip about the old Drake place, where Warren is building his home?"

"Just about everyone in town knows the old gold mine stories. But we also know there's nothing to them, that they're probably a myth." She shrugged her dainty, designer-clad shoulders. "That's about it."

"Gold?" Richard made sure that his face looked as skeptical as he sounded.

"Exactly. The story goes that a long time ago, like at least twenty-five, thirty years back, his grandfather, Walter Drake, and a partner found gold on their land. Some of the older citizens, including my grandmother, swear that they've seen nuggets that Walter himself showed them. But my mother doesn't believe there is any truth to the rumors, otherwise more of it would have been found by now, and by other people who have land in the surrounding area. So we think it's just one more part of what the elder Drake has tried to maintain as the Drake mystique."

"I find that story hard to believe myself. Like I said, me and Warren are tight, and he's never mentioned anything about gold on that land. So believe me, if there was any truth to the story, I'd know about it."

Even as he said this, he remembered the paperweight and what Warren had said: *Mined right in this part of the country.*

The waiter delivered his Parmesan chicken strips and her baked salmon. "Right now," he continued as he seasoned his entrée, "there's something else I'd like to know." Again, his voice had slid into that dreamy quality that he'd practiced on girls since puberty and honed over the years. "I want to know if a man like me can get a date with a girl like you. Because even if there was a ton of gold around here…you look like this place's most valuable treasure."

Chapter 21

Two days later, Warren sat in the front seat of his father's Lincoln, waiting curbside at Oakland International Airport to pick up his grandfather. They'd just pulled up when they saw the dark, distinguished gentleman pulling a carry-on bag.

Warren jumped out of the car. "There's the man!" He met his grandfather in the middle of the sidewalk and gave him a big hug. "Let's get you in the car and get going. At this airport they won't let you idle for long."

Once Walter was settled and buckled into the front seat and had exchanged greetings with Ike, he turned to Warren. "Did you remember what I told you before I left home?"

Warren chuckled. "You said that if you flew all the way out here and found nothing but gold dust to accompany that nugget, I'd owe you a thousand dollars *plus* all your expenses."

"Well, after all the fuss my wife made at me coming out here…make that two thousand dollars!"

The men laughed.

"How is Grandma Claire?" Warren asked.

"Yes, how is Mama doing?" Ike echoed. "Is she still in denial about her arthritis?"

"Your mama told me that there was only one man in her life, and his name wasn't Arthur!"

They burst into laughter again.

"She's doing pretty good. Still making those praline pies and spoiling Reginald's children." Reginald was the lone married child in Ike and Jennifer's clan, a point that Jennifer often made to the remaining siblings. "She also wants to know if y'all are all going to be down for Christmas."

"That's the plan."

"I told her before I left that we might have some gold to put under the tree. She told me not to hold my breath."

"Grandma Claire has always been pragmatic."

"Yes, her common sense has kept these old feet on the ground and money that otherwise might have been squandered gathering interest in the bank!"

The men continued talking while driving to the Drake family home, where Walter would freshen up, and then travel on to the site that he demanded to see before relaxing. Warren looked left and right as Ike Sr. drove down the long, tree-lined drive of Drake Ranch, still marveling that his dream of a home on this spot of land was so close to reality.

"This is it," he said proudly, placing a hand on his grandfather's shoulder. "The new and improved Drake Ranch."

"More like the one and only Drake Ranch, boy. Back when me and Charles owned it, it was called Northern California Dairy Farm."

"Gee, real creative, Grandpa," Warren drawled.

"We weren't as concerned about the name as the money it would produce," Walter countered.

"Let that be a lesson to you, son," Ike Sr. cautioned.

Warren could only nod in agreement.

They pulled up to the wide drive area, next to where a couple golf carts sat idle. Warren had phoned Jackson while Walter freshened up at his parents' house, so as soon as they drove up, he walked their way. Introductions were made before the men transferred to the golf cart and rode over to where the pool was being dug.

There, they met Jackson's subcontractor, Tom, who'd stayed behind to watch over the area…just in case.

"Good to meet you, Mr. Drake," Tom said as he removed his hard hat. "I think we might have something here. While y'all were gone, I took the liberty of sinking the bucket back down a time or two into the area where I'd found that first nugget. Then I handpicked through the dirt. Look what I found."

He opened his palm and revealed seven little rocks, similar to the one Warren had showed his dad.

"We're going to have to shut down your operation," Walter immediately said. "Get a security team over here, and a group of men that we can trust."

"You can trust Tom," Jackson said.

"Of course we can trust Jackson," Warren added.

"I'll only need five or six guys to dig," Tom stated, fixing his gaze on Walter. "But I have to tell you, sir, I don't know a thing about mining for gold."

Walter nodded. "That's why I'm here. If you've got the guys to work the machinery, I've got the knowledge to instruct them on what needs to be done. And a friend that I can call for backup. Won't take us more than four or five days to determine if this is a serious find or wishful thinking." He turned to Warren. "We're going to have to mess up more of your land, boy."

"No problem."

"And more than anything, we'll have to keep this quiet. Even with security, if the right amount of information gets heard by the wrong set of ears…there might be hell to pay."

Charli casually roamed the aisles of Paradise Cove's most upscale boutique. She wasn't interested in buying anything. No, this was the every-other-week girl time that Miss Alice insisted on having, or tried to, whenever Charli couldn't find a legitimate excuse to beg out of the affair. But she had to admit that for the first time in a long time she was showing more interest in the clothes on the rack and wondering whether or not Warren would appreciate seeing her in this or that outfit. Much to her chagrin.

Since he'd spent time with Griff at their house, she'd resisted the urge to contact him. As much as she'd wanted to. The night after his visit, she'd scoured her mind for a reason to call him. Two days later, she'd come close to driving over for a neighborly "do drop in." Yesterday, as her cows drank at the stream, she'd heard the sounds of heavy equipment and had almost ridden Butterscotch over to see the progress. He wouldn't have thought that forward… would he? In the end, she'd done nothing. Past memories and present insecurities had kept her away.

Charli wandered over to where Alice was admiring a beautiful navy blue suit. *As if she needs another.* There were more clothes still sporting price tags in her good friend's closet than should be legally allowed. Still, she knew how much Alice loved their outings, loved to gossip and loved to believe that she was impacting Charli's life. And she was. Alice and Charles had been good friends. Truth be told, Charli had come to believe that the two had been even closer than that. And given the fact that her and her mother's relationship was held together by long-distance calls, Alice was the closest female friend that

Charli had. So even as she was bored out of her gourd, she made a silent vow to herself to keep this in mind.

"Miss Alice. I think I'll go across the way and get some cash from the ATM. I'll be right back, okay?"

"That's fine, Charli." She held up two navy suits. "Which one looks better?"

"I like the one with the straight skirt," Charli said, pointing to her choice. "I think it would be flattering to your figure."

"I was thinking so, too. So I'll just purchase this one and meet you at the car."

"Sounds good."

Charli smiled at the nice salesclerk as she left the store. It was rare that she ventured into town but whenever she did, she was impressed by what Paradise Cove had done with this strip mall. Many times around the country they got a bad rap, but this one was classy. The nail salon was neat and clean, the dry cleaners eco-friendly, the coffee shop was a popular meeting spot for the town's elders and there wasn't a run-down building in sight. This was Paradise Cove, after all. Mostly, she loved the two businesses that anchored the spot: a family-owned grocery boasting organic and homegrown goodies and one of her favorite restaurants, Acquired Taste. The grocery store was where the ATM was located.

She headed over, humming softly, taking in the beautiful day and thinking about Warren. Again. She couldn't help it. Since he'd won over Griff, he'd been a constant presence—not only in her mind but in Griff's also. At least if their recent conversations were any indication. In the last week or so, they'd talked more about the dairy back when things were good, when Charles and Walter were friends. Griff had shared stories she'd never heard before about their legendary chess games and fishing excursions. They'd even talked about Charles's wife, Martha, the grandmother that Charli barely remembered because a car accident had taken her away too soon.

Just as she reached the grocery store, the last person in the world that she wanted to see was coming out.

Great. Just my luck. Of all the times and all the locations, I have to see you. In moments like these, Charli was reminded of just how small this town could be.

"Hello, beautiful." Cedric blocked her way inside the store.

"Move, Cedric." It was spoken in a voice that showed no love lost.

"What's your problem? You dissed me at the dance. You hung up when I called you. You're treating me like a piece of crap when you should be treating me like what I am, one of your oldest friends." Charli rolled her eyes and remained silent. "Do you seriously want me to believe that you're still fretting about something that happened a long time ago, back when we were kids?"

"I don't know, Cedric. How would you suggest I forget the night you tried to rape me?"

Chapter 22

"Rape you? Girl, you're overreacting."

"I don't think so." Once again, Charli tried to go around him. And once again, Cedric blocked her path.

"Cedric, I don't want to talk to you. Ever. Now move!"

"Not until we settle this little...misunderstanding. You're not the only one who remembers that night. Your grandfather's party, our families all happy, drinking and whatnot. You had on that cute little minidress, teasing me, flirting with me all night."

"You are such a liar. At the time my grandfather had that dance, animals were my best friends. Boys were the last thing on my mind."

"So you tried to get everyone to believe. But I knew you were hot to trot."

"Back then you were too ignorant to know much of anything." She looked him up and down with disdain. "I see nothing much has changed."

Cedric's eyes narrowed. He took a step closer.

Charli took a step back and placed a suggestive hand on her purse. Cedric didn't miss the gesture and backed up a bit.

"If you thought I tried to attack you, then why didn't you tell anybody? Why did you leave the barn, go back to the party and act as though nothing had occurred?"

"Because I was ashamed!" she spat, tears threatening to spill as memories escaped from where she'd locked them. "Because the last thing I wanted was for anyone else to know how *stupid* I'd been, how *naive* I was to believe that you actually wanted to come with me and see a baby colt!"

Cedric's laugh was low and sinister. "Baby, what I was looking for that night? I still want to see it."

This time it was Charli who took a step forward, anger guiding her moves. "Listen, you pigheaded jerk, and listen closely. I'm going to try one last time to penetrate that thick thing above your shoulders that usually houses a brain. Obviously not in your case but…here goes.

"I am not interested in you. I have never been interested in you and never will be. There is no part of the words *relationship, friendship* or *acquaintance* that I want to establish with you. If you were the last person on earth and held the last glass of water, I'd *die* rather than drink it. The only thing you are to me is someone that I used to know. And the best thing, the right thing and the *only* thing you can do for me is this. Leave. Me. Alone!"

With this, Charli pushed past him and placed her hand on the door handle.

"Bet you'd never say anything like that to Warren," Cedric snapped from behind her.

She whirled around. "Warren Drake has more class in his toenail than you do in your entire body."

She pushed open the door, entered the store and had no idea how long after she left Cedric continued to stand there, or the evil thoughts he vowed to see through to the end.

Later, Charli was still trying to calm down from the afternoon confrontation when her phone rang. When she didn't immediately recognize the number, she started not to answer it. Then she remembered that she'd blocked Cedric's number. And then she remembered something else: to whom this number belonged.

She snatched up the phone. "Hello?"

"Hey, there you are. I was all prepared to leave a message."

"Hey, Drake." The fact that just hearing his voice helped calm her nerves was not lost on her.

"Sounds like I caught you in the middle of something. You sound out of breath."

"I'm all right. Just rushed to grab the phone. What's up?"

"I just wanted to warn you that we'll be doing some extensive excavating over the next few days. Might come real close to the property line, maybe dig up some of your land. We'll fix any part of your place that gets damaged. Also wanted to make sure that you still had a key to the gate, since the electricity might be out during the process."

She plopped down on her bed, glad to have her mind distracted by mundane, everyday matters, such as things that concerned the ranch. "What's up with all the digging?"

"A couple of things. One of which is that the crew that's laying pipe that will be connected to my in-ground pool wants to check out the surrounding grounds, make sure there are no craters or sand traps that can later become sinkholes."

Charli almost shuddered as she remembered the recent news story about a sinkhole that opened up in Southern California and swallowed a whole house. "Do you think that's possible? That we have sinkholes around us?"

"I don't want to believe it. But I also want to keep us safe."

Us. She knew it shouldn't, but the way he'd used that word made her feel warm and cozy. Like he had at least some of her best interests at heart. Like maybe in one way or another, just a little, she mattered. *Silly girl.*

"Charli?"

His voice was soft and low, pouring over like warm, soapy water, or the sweet, sticky molasses that Griff so enjoyed. Her muscles clenched, her thong became wet and she thought of things that happened between a woman and a man when clothes were not an option.

"Yes?"

"Are you all right?"

He'd said it so sincerely, as if he had a stake in asking, as if he really wanted to know. So before she could think or rationalize or put on her superwoman cape and feign indifference, she answered honestly. "No."

"What's wrong?"

She told him about the confrontation, about what had happened earlier between her and Cedric. A shorter, more sanitized version, leaving out the bit about parties and barns and near sexual assaults. "He terrorized me when we were younger," she explained. "I've never liked him."

"I don't, either." Warren's words were short, curt, delivered in anger. "Just say the word and I'll have a talk with him. I hate when a so-called man tries to intimidate someone of the weaker sex."

"I'm not weak!" Charli retorted, her hackles raised at once at the mere suggestion. "Just because I've been vulnerable does not mean I've been weak."

"Sorry, baby, poor choice of words. Dang, my bad. 'Baby' might also be offensive. I mean no harm, Charli. I'm on your side."

"I believe that. And I just may be a tad hypersensitive."

"You think?"

She laughed at the humor in his voice. "I've grown up holding the banner for women while surrounded by men."

"You've done a great job." A companionable silence ensued for a few seconds and then, "Charli, where are your parents, if you don't mind me asking? I was thinking about you the other day and realized that there is so much that I do not know."

She knew that she should hedge, that she should put her guard up to this blatant request for personal information. But for the life of her she couldn't find a defensive bone in her body. She was too busy smiling at the fact that he'd been thinking about her.

"Better yet, why don't we both take a break and go riding? I haven't had Coal out all day and could use the fresh air. What about you?"

"That sounds like a great idea, Drake."

"Good. I'll be at your place in about five minutes."

Charli listened as Griff's hard-heeled boots scraped the hardwood floor. Even though they'd shared a bonding moment, she knew that Griff still held it against him that Warren was a Drake. "Why don't we meet down by the fence instead?"

"See you there."

Several minutes later, Warren watched the fluid motions of horse and rider as Charli rode up to meet him. She wore no cowboy hat today. Instead, her natural curls bounced in the wind, along with lush breasts straining against a pastel-yellow tee. He took in khakis molding her thighs and felt his passion rise. She was wild and free, like the countryside. He couldn't remember having seen a more beautiful sight in his life.

"Hey," she said when she pulled along beside him.

"Hello, Charli."

"Where do you want to ride?"

"Why don't you take the lead? You know this land better than I do."

"I do, don't I?" He'd barely caught the sparkle of mischief in her eyes before she turned the reins, tapped her palomino and took off. "Yah!"

Warren burst out laughing as he took off after her. She obviously still remembered how he'd beaten her during that first impromptu race and wanted to even the score. He had no problem letting her stay ahead. It gave him a chance to appreciate how well she was wearing those pants, how her butt lifted rhythmically with the gait of the horse, how her hair blew in the wind and how he wanted to wrap his arms around her slender waist and not let go.

For several minutes the only sounds were horse hooves hitting hard dirt. As they entered a wide expanse of land, framed by a cloudless blue sky, vibrant green grass and a copse of trees on one side, Warren gave Coal the signal and the horse shot forward, easily catching up to Charli and her horse.

"Still trying to beat me, huh?" Warren shouted, as they matched each other stride for stride.

"A girl can dream!" Charli laughed, and to Warren it sounded like joy and felt like fairy dust. It transported him to his childhood, when he was young, life was fun and there wasn't a care in the world. She turned down a dirt lane, one that Warren hadn't even known was there. It was as if they'd been transported to another world as large trees bordered the road on both sides, their branches so large and leafy that it created a shady canopy—or, as they slowed their horses to a trot and Warren took in the natural beauty beside him, a lovers' haven.

They reached a part of the fence that was indented, built around a large oak tree. Charli turned her horse into the space, dismounted and looped the reins around the top of a protruding board. Warren followed suit.

Warren looked at his surroundings, and then back at Charli. "Beautiful."

"It is, isn't it? I used to spend hours here, felt it was my own personal paradise."

"The landscape is lovely, but that's not what I meant." He took a step closer. "You're beautiful, Charli."

Charli took a step back and came up against the fence. Her chest rose and fell rapidly and Warren could see the quickened pulse on her neck. She licked her lips nervously. It was Warren's undoing, bringing back a rush of memories. Another time. That first caress. He quickly closed the distance between them and, without a word or a second's hesitation, pressed his lips against Charli's as his arms went around her. When she opened her mouth to protest, he took full advantage, sliding his tongue inside her moist sweetness. A moan escaped her mouth. Warren caught it, swallowed it and deepened the kiss—pressing his body full against her, his pelvis beginning a familiar dance on its own.

For a few blissful seconds, Charli's mind was totally detached from her body, causing her not to think, but to feel. And what a feast of feeling stood before her: from the broad shoulders her hands sculpted to the strong back they slid down, all while experiencing the most delicious kiss she'd ever felt. Unlike other men she'd known, Warren's wasn't so much a kiss as a collision. The way his tongue swirled lazily with hers and his head rotated to match his pelvis.

Through her haze, she felt a piece of wood that was harder than the planks against her back and butt. This human woody fairly pulsated against her abdomen and brought moisture to her sex as it was ground against her. She began to shake with the intensity of her attraction, began to feel as though she were being pulled into a vortex from which there would be no return.

With the last vestiges of sanity and control…she broke the kiss.

But Warren would not let her break his hold. "Charli," he whispered, his tongue darting out to touch her ear. "There's something between us. I know you feel it, too."

"It's rather hard to miss," was her dry reply.

Warren chuckled. "Not only this," he said, nudging her with his rock-hard penis. "But also these feelings, this thing between us. I don't just want to have sex with you, I want to date you. I want us to ride out this attraction and see where it leads."

"I'm not sure I'm ready."

Warren released her and took a step back. "We'll go as slow as you'd like."

"Are you sure you can wait that long?" Charli's eyes searched his, trying to read his mind as well as hear his words.

Warren's eyes narrowed as he slowly perused her body, going from her head to her feet and back up again. He noted the hardened nipples straining against her T-shirt, her moist, kiss-swollen lips, her flushed face and the desire in her eyes.

His smile was bright, his eyes knowing as he answered her question with one of his own. "Can you?"

Chapter 23

Warren stood to the side of the large hole. He watched his grandfather, obviously in his element, converse with the gold-mining expert he'd phoned and brought to the site. Walter, decked out in hard hat and blue jeans, rubber boots and a cotton shirt, laughed at something the expert said and Warren smiled. It was clear that calling his grandfather had been the right thing to do. Walter Drake often boasted about how much he loved retirement, but he also loved people. Looking at him now, Warren knew that interacting in this type of productive fashion was something that his grandfather missed.

It was just as well that Walter was here, and in control. Because try as he might, even with the prospect of finding the proverbial pot of gold at the end of the rainbow before him, all he could think about was Charli and yesterday evening's conversation, the one they'd had on the way back from their spontaneous tryst in the woods. Even now it replayed in his mind.

* * *

"Tell me about your parents."

Charli had hesitated only a moment before answering. "They divorced when I was little. Dad remarried, had two more children—my younger half brother and sister—and lives in Hawaii. My mother started dating Pierre when I was thirteen. That's when I began spending most of my time at Grandpa's ranch. They married when I was sixteen and I moved in with Grandpa until it was time for college."

"Why didn't you stay with your mother? Did you not like Pierre?"

"He tried as best he could, but I probably wouldn't have liked anyone my mother brought into my life. I'd been a huge daddy's girl, just adored my father. It hurt me deeply when he left, seemingly without a backward glance. It was years later when I learned that his new wife had a lot to do with it, that she was always jealous of my mother, and afraid he'd go back to her. And since I am part of my mother, she was jealous of me, too. To say that she didn't encourage a continued relationship is putting it mildly.

"But by the time Pierre and my mom married, I'd accepted their relationship and become somewhat cordial. He's from Canada, though, and when they made the decision to move back there, I chose to stay. I'd become as close to my grandfather as I'd once been to my dad."

"Did I ever meet your mother?"

"Cherise Reed? Probably not. We lived in Oakland. But you might have seen her picture. She used to model, and appeared quite frequently in *Ebony, Essence* and other magazines. Her most popular picture is the one where she is wearing strips of colorful, carefully placed strips of cloth…and not much else."

"I remember!" Warren had said after a moment of thinking. "Very regal, looked a little like that other dark-skinned model…what's her name?"

"Iman. Yes, you've remembered. My mom actually did a few shows with Iman, in Paris and Milan. But that was before she married and had children."

"Children as in plural? You have a sibling outside of your half brother and sister?"

"No, I don't. My mom became pregnant with what would have been my younger sister. But she was stillborn."

"I'm sorry."

"It's okay. I was only four years old and don't remember."

"Charli," Warren had asked once they reached the gate where their ride had begun and they'd stilled the horses.

"Yes?"

"I asked Griff and he wouldn't tell me. But do you know what happened between our grandfathers?"

"I know what my grandfather and Griff have told me. But your grandfather is still living, right?"

"Yes."

"Then I'd have to agree with Griff on this one. I think that you should ask him."

As he watched Walter wave him over to where the men now gathered, Warren considered Charli's suggestion to ask him what happened. Before his grandfather left California for New Orleans, he vowed to do just that.

"We've got a situation," Walter said as soon as Warren reached them.

"What's happening?"

"The way things are looking, we need to dig horizontally instead of vertically." Walter's face was fixed in a frown as he delivered this news.

Warren shrugged. "Fine with me."

"Not so fine, grandson."

"It's our land. What's the problem?"

Walter looked at the man he'd known since his gold heyday, the expert he'd flown up from his retirement home in Florida.

"This device here," Mr. Sanders said, "tracks gold. We put it on the end of a prod and send it into the ground for readings. We've been doing that all morning and the more we dig westward—" the man pointed toward Charli's farm "—the louder she pings."

"Ah," Warren said, as Walter's concerns dawned. "You think the gold might run all the way onto Reed property."

Walter scowled. "Precisely. And I sure hope that that is not the case."

"Why, Grandpa? I'll just alert Charli and Griff that there's—"

"Griff?" Walter interrupted. "Is that mean hound still living?"

Hmm, that conversation about Charles Reed and the ranch may take place sooner than I thought. "Yes, Grandpa. He's very much alive. He and Charles Reed's granddaughter still have the farm and still run the dairy."

"Well, the last thing you want is to get them involved in this. If Griff gets a sniff of money about, there's no telling what he'll do."

Warren looked at the curious expressions of Jackson, Tom, Mr. Retirement and the crew and then looked at his grandfather. "Let's take a ride," he said, already turning to walk away. "I need you over here."

He walked fast, knew that his grandfather was working to keep up, but kept moving. When he reached the SUV he popped the lock and climbed inside.

Walter was right behind him. "What's going on, Warren? You left those men like the devil was after you. What's over here that I need to see?"

Warren turned to face him. "A different perspective."

"Excuse me?"

"Or at least I do. When I first took an interest in this

property, I had no concern about or knowledge of my neighbors. Then, when I put up the property fence, I met Charli, Charles's granddaughter. She was rude and full of attitude."

"You said she was kin to Charles, right? You've heard that saying about apples and trees."

"Later," Warren continued, pointedly ignoring his grandfather, "I met Griff and got more of the same."

"Surprised you didn't get filled with buckshot," Walter mumbled.

"But a few weeks ago, after yet another misunderstanding, I went over to their house." Walter looked at him, aghast. "We talked about what was bothering me and settled some things. I'm proud to say that as of right now, we're cordial neighbors, I'd even say friends. But that's not why I pulled you away from the group."

Walter was silent, possibly still digesting Warren's surprising words. "You wanted to tell me about your new friendships?" he finally asked with more than a little sarcasm.

"No. I want you to tell me about your past enemy. Specifically, I want to know what happened between you and Charles Reed."

Chapter 24

"I need to see you."

Five simple words that caused Charli to unexpectedly exercise her core muscle. It had been two days since their horse ride, and Coal's rider had been all she'd thought about. Him, the kiss and the impossibility of it all.

"I'm rather busy," she responded after a pause. "We've got a man coming by to give an estimate on fixing the water tank and Bobby just discovered a hole in the fence that—"

"Charli. Stop."

She knew she was prattling but with the myriad of thoughts and emotions chasing themselves around her brain, it was the best she could do.

"Five or ten minutes is all I need." She continued to hesitate. "It's important."

"Are you at the ranch?"

"Yes."

"I'll be there in half an hour."

Charli pulled her Ford up next to Warren's shiny new SUV. She'd purposely covered her ripped tank top and jeans with an oversize striped shirt, then knotted it at the waist. Unbeknownst to her, what she called modesty Warren would find as sexy as sin.

Looking around and not seeing Warren, she exited the truck and walked up to the man she'd seen on both of her previous visits to the ranch.

"Excuse me." The man turned around. "I'm looking for Drake."

The man's brow rose slightly. "Warren?" She nodded. He smiled. "Charli, right?" Another nod. He held out his hand. "Hi, I'm Jackson Wright, Warren's brother-in-law." They shook hands. "He's in his office." He pointed to a building not far from the stables. "His office is at the end of the hall. I think his secretary may be at lunch, so if she's not at her desk, go on back."

"Thanks."

Charli walked across the gravel drive to a simple A-frame building painted a stark white with black trim. Here, a concrete sidewalk had been poured, leading up to the door. She entered and after seeing the desk facing the door empty, continued down the hall.

"Drake?"

"Back here."

She stopped, took a deep breath and then proceeded to the open door at the end of the hall. "Hello."

"Hello, sexy neighbor."

Doing her best to ignore the compliment, she took a moment to look around his office and get her feelings in check. The plainness of the outside was deceiving. Inside, Drake's office looked rich and inviting: floors made of ebony wood with the same wood used for the built-in bookcases only half-filled with books. In contrast his desk was modern, made mostly of smoky glass, and devoid of anything save an iPad and the folder he was perusing. On his tan-colored walls were framed enlarged photographs of what appeared to be an aerial view of the property, a wide shot of his vineyards and a close-up picture of a cluster of grapes. There were also two framed diplomas and a black-and-white photo of a young man in overalls standing next to a tractor.

She observed all this in a matter of seconds before saying, "What do you need to see me about, Drake? As I said on the phone, I don't have much time." She looked at her watch for emphasis.

Warren leaned back against the plush black swivel chair in which he sat. "Are you going to act defensive every time you see me, even after the other day?"

"I'm not defensive," she stated, very defensively.

"Ha! What would you call it?"

"I'd call it direct, to the point. Which, if you don't get to it…" She turned slightly.

"Slow your roll, Charli. Close the door and have a seat." She looked skeptically at the door, then back at him.

"Don't worry, I won't bite you." She began shutting the door. "At least not without your permission." She stopped. He laughed. "Please."

She offered her style of smile, a smirk, really, before she closed the door, walked over to one of two black leather chairs facing Warren's desk and sat down.

"You remember the digging I told you about, how we might have to extend it onto your property?"

"Yes."

"Well, that's no longer a possibility, but a definite."

She frowned. "You had to see me for that? I already told you that as long as you repaired what you tore up, it was okay."

"That's not all. It's not only that we're digging up your land, it's now why."

"You found a sinkhole?"

"No, Charli. We've found gold."

"Gold?"

"Yes."

"Here, on our land?"

"Yes." He stood, walked over to one of the bookshelves and reached for a small, covered porcelain bowl, then walked over and handed it to Charli. "Take a look," he said, walking back to his chair and sitting down.

She took off the lid, set it on the smoky glass table between the two chairs, then spilled the collection of rocks into her hand. "These are rocks."

"At first glance that's what anyone would think. But those are gold nuggets, darling. And according to my expert grandfather, there is plenty more where that came from—some of which is on your property."

Charli studied the rocks more carefully. "This is gold?"

"Yep."

"How much do you think there is? I mean, could there be enough to…"

"End your financial worries? We don't know. But there is enough to warrant us digging deeper and finding out. That's why I needed to see you. I know the bad blood that has existed between our families and want everything about this joint venture to be legal and aboveboard. I also want us to split any profits fifty-fifty."

"With you handling time, labor and all up-front expenses, how can we do that?"

"We can do it because it's the only arrangement I'll accept."

She shook her head. "No can do, Drake. If this is a joint venture, then my say counts, too. And I'd say that with your gifting the cows you've already done too much. For this to feel right, I've got to share some of the financial burden of the excavation."

Tension whipped around in the silence like errant particles of dust across Warren's glass desk. "If you insist," Warren finally answered with a shrug.

"I do. And I need to run any paperwork past Griff and our own set of lawyers."

"Of course." Warren fully intended to pay for everything concerning the excavation, a point he felt was best kept to himself until he could persuade her to his way of thinking. "Anything else?"

"Not that I can think of at the moment."

"I'll have my attorneys get right on this and send over something as soon as possible, perhaps as early as tomorrow morning."

"Okay."

Warren stood and walked toward her. Charli stood, too. "Now," he said, his voice low and husky as he stood in front of her. "Was what I just shared worth your time in coming over?"

Kicking herself for licking her lips after eyeing his succulent ones, she answered, "Yes."

"One more question."

"Shoot."

"Can I bite you?" She shyly shook her head. "No?"

"No," she said softly. "No biting."

"Then may I have a kiss?"

"Yes."

"Two?"

"Don't push it."

Warren had no intention of pushing it, or of continuing the conversation at all. One more look at her luscious lips and he knew that there were much better ways that they could be spending this time alone.

Chapter 25

A week after Warren's conversation with his grandfather and the subsequent conversation with Charli, a lot had happened. So much so that Warren felt he needed to get away from everything and everybody just to sort it all out. And he wanted Charli to go with him. That's why he'd called her last night and asked her out to dinner. He'd said nothing more than to wear slacks and bring a jacket. And that's why she now stood on a wide expanse of land about ten miles out of town with the sound of helicopter blades whirring around them and a look of surprise on her face.

"I've never been in a helicopter before," she shouted over the humming propellers.

"I've only been up a few times myself," Warren admitted. He looked across the strip at the pilot, who nodded and gave him a thumbs-up. Warren took Charli's arm. "Let's go!"

They entered the helicopter and within minutes had

been outfitted with the devices through which they could communicate and be heard over the roar.

"This is crazy!" Charli said, her eyes bright, excited. "When you asked me out to dinner I was thinking either Acquired Taste or Bucks!"

Bucks was the second most popular eatery in Paradise Cove. As down-home as Acquired Taste was upscale, the establishment boasted barbecued ribs, succulent fried chicken and the best burgers in town.

"I didn't want anyone to see us!" Immediately realizing how that must have sounded, he touched her arm and added, "Wait, that didn't come out right. I'd love for people to know I'm with the prettiest girl in Paradise Cove. I just don't want people even more in our business than they are already!"

"Thanks for being kind. But we both know that you're talking about Griff."

"I have to give it to the old man. When it comes to you, he's very protective. Though I'm hoping that after your lawyers have reviewed and approved the contract, he'll stop being suspicious."

Charli laughed. "He'll stop being suspicious of you when you stop being a Drake."

"Unfortunately, you're probably right. Wish he'd had that same kind of suspicion when his friend showed up before asking for the man's opinion—" Warren made air quotes "—in confidence."

It was true. Upon hearing about the gold and the proposed Drake/Reed joint venture, a highly wary Griff had asked the advice of a longtime friend who'd just happened to drop by their farm the same day that Charli had shared the news. One thing led to another and Griff's friend told his wife, who then shared it with her beautician at one of the town's hair salons. That had been the beginning of the end of their secret gold find. Now what was happening on the Drake and Reed properties was the talk of Paradise Cove.

"Where are we going?" she asked.

"San Francisco, baby."

"Oh, really? Cool! I've only been back a few times since graduating Berkeley."

Casual conversation continued during the thirty-minute ride to a San Francisco airstrip. Once there, a town car awaited to whisk them into the heart of the city and to the chic restaurant Jackson had told Warren about. There was one stop before that, however. It was to a chic downtown boutique, close to the city's financial district. It wasn't until they were comfortably seated at the private booth that they both felt they could truly catch their breaths.

Charli picked up her glass of lemon water. "Wow, that helicopter ride was exciting."

"It was pretty nice. And may I say, you look lovely."

Charli eased a hand over the silky, formfitting dress that both the saleswoman and Warren had talked her into letting him buy. "It is as if both the color and design were made for you," the woman had vowed in heavily accented English. She was right. The one-shoulder number that boasted a subtle butterfly print against a primarily coral background emphasized her neck and toned arms, while the cut highlighted her ample breasts, slender waist and long legs. The dress stopped a couple inches above her knees. Its color complemented her deeply tanned skin perfectly, a coppery tone further enhanced by the bronzer brush of the makeup artist whose shop was next door to the boutique. Finally, a dainty pair of strappy, jeweled heels, along with teardrop earrings and a bracelet of Swarovski crystals and a light shawl completed her ensemble. There was no denying it: when Charli left the shop she'd felt like Cinderella.

She still did.

"If you were trying to make an impression…mission accomplished." This statement was accompanied by the almost smile that Warren now expected.

"Believe it or not, woman, I'm just trying to have some peace!"

"Ha! Well, for the record, you clean up pretty well yourself."

Warren smiled. "Thank you."

He wasn't the cocky sort but had been told more than once how he blessed a pair of slacks or jeans. He'd kept his attire simple: black suit, stark white shirt, pinstriped tie of black, gray and coral. He'd visited his barber first thing that morning and knew his close-cropped curls looked just right. Never one for much flash, he limited his accessories to an understated Cartier watch and monogrammed platinum cuff links.

"Seriously, I'm glad for this time with just the two of us. This situation is getting crazy. Various family members have suddenly becoming mining experts, my parents are now the most popular guests on the dinner circuit and the final straw? A call from a reporter at the *Cove Chronicle,* wanting a quote."

"She called you, too?"

Warren nodded. "If I'd known it was going to get like this, I might have kept that little nugget in my pocket and never called Grandpa."

"All this hoopla on the mere *chance* that there might be serious gold down there." She shook her head, her eyes wistful. "I never in a million years would have thought that gold existed under my cattle's hooves. Like you, I've grown up with the stories. Except mine were tinged with my grandfather's intense…dislike for your grandfather."

Warren sighed. "I think that unfortunately there was some mutual dislike going on."

"You told me that you asked him about what happened between them. But you never shared what he said."

Charli had been curious when she'd heard that *the* Walter Drake, the man she'd heard so much about from her grandfather, was back in town. "You don't have to. It's…"

"Not important," Warren finished.

They paused while the waiter came out, freshened their waters and took drink and food orders. When he left, Warren continued. "The fact of the matter is what happened between those two men is in the past and has nothing to do with us. I believe that even if my grandfather did have a problem with Charles Reed, it was his problem. I don't have to make it mine. After talking with my grandfather, that's what I decided."

Charli was quiet for a moment, looking at Warren with an unreadable expression. "I never looked at it quite that way."

Warren gave her a crooked smile, making him appear boyish and unassuming. "I got that feeling."

"Stop it!" She slapped his wrist, and for the first time since they'd met, gave him a genuine smile.

"You should do that more often."

"What?"

"Smile." Taking a huge chance, he reached for her hand, held it between his two large ones before exposing her palm and running a strong, thick forefinger down her lifeline. Taking an even bigger chance…he kissed her.

It was a definable moment when their lips touched, when he applied the merest pressure before pulling back, looking into her eyes and then kissing her once more.

She didn't back away. Somehow he knew she wouldn't. It was as if being in a different place, away from all that was familiar and those who knew them oh so well, allowed a different side of each of them to be explored.

Allowed them to enjoy the attraction that Charli tried so hard to deny.

For him, it was a side that pushed away worries about ulterior motives or rejection, two issues that had dogged past relationships.

For her, it was a side that embraced the concept of trust, in a man, but even more importantly, in herself.

"That was nice," he finally said.

"Yes," she said, dipping her head in a moment of shyness. "It was."

For a brief snatch of time they just sat there in a companionable silence, each dealing with their own thoughts, feelings and reactions. In the end, the look they gave each other said that there would be no going back to whatever they had before. They'd just gone to another level. And both were happy about that.

The waiter brought their salads and soon gushing comments about the deliciousness of their meal vied with personal bits and pieces that allowed Warren and Charli to know each other more. There were more smiles and laughter than they'd ever previously shared. By the time the entrées arrived, a new understanding had been reached.

"I'm so glad the legalities regarding the Drake/Reed excavation are behind us. Although I wish you'd stop fighting it and let my company absorb the expenses. I was putting in an in-ground pool, remember? So an excavation would have occurred at any rate."

In a rare show of flirtation, Charli leaned forward. She used her newly manicured fingernail to graze the back of Warren's hand. While looking up into his eyes, she purred, "I thought you brought me all the way up here so we could stop talking about the gold rush."

Warren's eyes went from looking at hers to observing her lips, licking his own as he remembered the kiss. "I know what I'd like to do." Warren's phone rang. "Hold that thought." He pulled it from his pocket. "The pilot," he mouthed to Charli as he took the call. "Hello?" He nodded, then frowned. "Seriously?" He muted the phone. "A problem with the helicopter I rented. They're trying to find another one to take us home." He returned to the call. "Yes, I'm here. Uh-huh. We just finished dinner and are about to have dessert." He listened for another minute and then asked Charli an unexpected question. Perhaps it had something to do with his growing courage and her emboldened flirtations.

"By the time they either fix or replace the helicopter, it will be midnight or later. Do you want to just spend the night here, in San Francisco?"

Charli's answer was even more unexpected, for both of them. "Yes."

Chapter 26

They were in the heart of San Francisco, in the Civic Center Plaza, near Market Street and San Francisco's widest thoroughfare, Van Ness. Warren spoke with the waiter, who brought over the maître d', who suggested a hotel very near their establishment. An hour later, after enjoying decadent desserts and after-dinner drinks, they arrived at a beautiful suite bearing a rather ironic name considering where Warren's parents lived: the Mandarin Oriental Hotel's Golden Gate suite.

"This is stunning," Charli said as she entered the large, elegantly appointed set of rooms with large windows that offered stunning, unobstructed views of San Francisco's twinkling skyline and a bird's-eye view of the majestic Golden Gate Bridge. She turned to Warren, her eyes bright and shiny, like those of a child with a new toy. "I've never been in a place so beautiful before."

"I'm just sorry about the circumstances that put us here," Warren said. "My family has used that helicopter company for several years and nothing has ever happened like this. I'm really sorry."

"Drake, quit apologizing." She walked over and stood directly in front of him. "It's okay."

He tried not to react to the look in her eyes, to that mixture of wonder, gratitude and…absolute trust? It made his heart flip-flop and caused stirrings below. In this moment he realized the impossibility and danger of this situation: one very soft, very big bed; no luggage, meaning no night clothes; a romantic setting and one of the most beautiful women he'd ever met. In that moment Warren knew that if this scenario didn't end with his making slow, sweet love to her…it was going to be a very long night.

He took a step. "May I kiss you again?"

She nodded.

It began with just their lips touching: soft, tender, reserved. But when Warren reached out and pulled her flush against him and Charli gasped, the experience quickly turned hot. Warren darted his tongue into her open mouth, which still tasted of chocolate and berried wine. She groaned and it set him on fire, bringing out all of the longing from his months without sex, from feelings that had been hidden, for a date with destiny that wouldn't be denied. He shifted his head to go even deeper, to taste more of her—cheek, temple, nose, ear—but it was still not enough.

Obviously the feeling was mutual because Charli reached up and put her arms around his neck, going up on tiptoe to deepen their exchange. Their bodies began to rub against each other. His hand moved down the length of her back, enjoying the satiny fabric of her fancy dress before touching the perfectly shaped, firm butt that had driven him crazy on more than one occasion. He grabbed and squeezed and she moaned aloud. The sound sent blood gushing to the tip of his shaft, his tool like a raging python straining for relief from its cage. If something wasn't done soon, he would burst.

He knew what could tame the python, what could soothe the beast. He was holding her in his arms.

"Charli," he whispered against her mouth. They stopped, forehead to forehead, both panting for breath and a return from a moment when they'd both lost track of reality, had both become lost in the pleasure of a simple kiss. Except that was just it—because it had happened between Warren and Charli, nothing about it was simple. The kiss seemed to weave a web around them, draw them together in a way that was inexplicable yet undeniable.

It was true, and both knew it when they raised their heads and looked into each other's eyes.

"Earlier," Charli began, her voice a whisper as she still panted slightly, "down at the table, you said that you wanted to do something. Right before the pilot called. Do you remember?"

He nodded. "We just did what I was thinking about down there. But there's something else." He eased a finger between them, over the bodice of her dress to the dip that emphasized her cleavage until he reached the outline of her hardened nipple and tweaked it, all the while looking deep into her eyes.

She swallowed, her breath coming in short bursts. "What?"

"I want to make love to you. Would you like that?"

"It's been awhile for me. I don't know if I can satisfy you or—"

"Shh, don't even go there. You are beautiful. You are perfect. And everything about you turns me on."

On those words, they raced into another kiss: tongues swirling, bodies touching, hearts beating as one. And all the while Warren's beast kept growing, throbbing.

This time it was Charli who broke the kiss, reaching

up to run her tongue around his ear before she whispered, "You're so hard."

"Uh-huh."

She slid her hand over his trousers. "Oh my God."

He hissed. "Baby, I'm about to burst."

"Well, we can't have that," she said, stepping away from him. "Shall we take a shower first?"

His answer was to lead them into the master bath.

They disrobed on the way, clothes dropping wherever they were pulled off. By the time they reached the marble masterpiece, both were naked.

Warren's irises darkened as he looked at her. "You're more beautiful than I imagined."

Charli looked down. "And you're...bigger than I feared."

For Warren, a rumble of laughter bubbled just below the surface.

"I'm serious. Is that thing registered, because it is definitely a lethal weapon!"

"Ha!"

She joined in the laughter and her jesting took some of the tension and nervousness out of the moment. Warren started the water and once it reached the right temperature, they stepped in. As soon as he ran his fingers over her nipples, following the water droplets down her body to the V-shaped paradise below, things became serious again.

He leaned in, kissed her, even as he continued to rub against her with his finger, until she relaxed and spread her legs farther apart, inviting him in. He continued rubbing steadily, rhythmically, until her pelvis picked up the melody and joined the dance. His tongue swirled to match this beat and soon Charli pressed her hand against his, wanting more.

It was what he wanted, too. He placed a finger inside her, and then another. Flicking his thumb over her hardening nub, he lazily rubbed his hand between her dewy folds. He felt her muscles contract against his fingers, an act that hardened him even more. He hoped that she was ready for him, because he couldn't wait. Not one. More. Second. He lifted her up amid the sprays from multiple jets and placed her against the cool tile. When he stepped immediately between her legs, she wrapped them around his waist. Her nipple was right where he wanted it—directly in front of his mouth. He sucked it in, then nipped and licked, driving her into a frenzy. Reaching down between them, he grabbed his dick and placed the tip against her.

She moaned.

"Are you ready?"

"Yes," she eked out between breaths. "Please."

He pushed ever so slightly, noticed the resistance and backed away. Over and over again, he teased her with his tip, infinitely patient, amazingly gentle. Inch by delicious thick inch until she again began to move her body, encouraging him to go where he wanted, to take what he needed.

"More!"

Oh, yeah. He lifted her a little higher, pulled out to the tip and then slid in, but this time he was able to take it all… the…way. *Umm.* For a moment they were still, her adjusting to the throbbing gift inside her, him relishing the feel of her tight delight. Then the dance began in earnest: hips gyrating, pelvis thrusting, kissing breasts and mouth and neck and wherever their mouths could land.

The thrusting continued: hard, rhythmic, fast, slow, in, out, ahh. Charli felt a swirling sensation building up inside her, a yearning that threatened to take her over the edge. Tears sprang to her eyes as she gripped his shoulders. He sensed the nearness of her release, stepped back, grabbed her hips and pounded. Methodically. Deliciously. Until she burst.

Her legs were still shaking, still wobbly as he turned her around and entered her once again. He feasted upon the pert, round ass he loved so much, became acquainted with every aspect of it as he pushed toward his own climatic finish. And when it came he felt that he'd exploded into a thousand pieces—with Charli's name engraved on every single one.

Chapter 27

Farmers got up early, and Charli was no exception. So even though she was in a pricey hotel suite instead of the back bedroom on Reed Ranch, her eyes opened shortly after the sun came up. She shifted, felt a strong, long leg pressing against hers and instantly everything came back from the night before. Lying there, staring at the ceiling, a wave of emotions overcame her. Jumbled thoughts fought for dominance in her brain. She'd just experienced the most magical night of her life. So why did she feel so bad about it?

Because try as she might to change deeply ingrained feelings and beliefs, they still persisted. She'd slept with the enemy.

With a sigh, she rolled out of bed and headed to the luxurious bathroom, the same one that last night had been a backdrop for heart-stopping sex. Now she could barely look at the tub where the delicious decadence had continued after their time in the shower. She walked into the large, tiled shower stall, turned the water on full force, as hot as she could stand it. Her head went under the powerful showerhead and soon tears joined the water pouring down her face. She stayed that way, confused, thinking. Her rational mind said otherwise but years of conditioning made her feel as though she'd let her grandfather down.

She sensed Warren's presence and seconds later, felt the draft from the shower door opening.

"May I join you?"

His voice was deep and a bit raspy from sleep. She closed her eyes, her mind conjuring up an image of how he must look: towering, toned, rock-hard and ready.

She squeezed her eyes tight and cleared her throat, hoping that she could speak and not choke on a sob.

Without turning around, barely moving, she uttered, "Umm…I'll be out in a minute."

A long pause and then, "Okay."

The soft click of the shower door closing felt like a dagger in her heart. No matter what her grandfather had told her about his family, no matter how the man who she thought hung the sun and the moon had felt about his ex-partner, that partner's grandson, Warren Drake, had been nothing but kind, honest and amazing to her.

Highfalutin city slicker.

Self-absorbed, bourgie possums.

"That's what Grandpa would say," she whispered. And then there was Griff. *Nothing in life is free. Have you considered that money may not be the means of exchange he has in mind?* He'd said it after Warren bought the cows and reiterated it during their conversation about the gold, adding that with the Drakes' money and influence, not even that contract could be trusted. Reaching for the shampoo, she worked the frothy lather into her hair. Another voice spoke into her conscience—her own. *How has he treated you? What have you seen?*

A thoughtful neighbor, who'd put a gate in his fence and given her both the code and key even when he didn't have to.

A generous soul who when she'd lost one cow had replaced it with two.

A spontaneous man who scheduled a fun helicopter ride into a fabulous city and treated her like a queen.

A skilled lover who'd played her like an instrument, who'd pleasured her body while touching her soul.

Convincing actions, but memories of another man—Charles Reed—continued to leave her tormented. How could she be disloyal to his memory by being with someone from the family he'd so despised? When her father had left to pursue a new relationship, and when her mother had eventually gone on to do the same, it had been her grandfather, Charles Reed, who'd remained the constant in her life. Who'd nurtured her confidence and helped raise her self-esteem. While some little girls might have been with their moms baking or hitting the mall, Charli had been on the farm feeding chickens and learning to shoot. Other children had cats for pets. Charli had cows. Almost every person save her dear grandfather, Griff and their friend Miss Alice had let her down. And certainly every romantic interest. *Until Warren.* Torn didn't begin to describe her emotions. Then it hit her, the crux of her dilemma.

Charli would have to decide whether she wanted to embrace the present, or live in the past.

Something was wrong. *But what?* Warren pulled on the fluffy white robe the hotel provided and walked to the window. Wisps of color—orange, red and various blues—announced a new day. The city below was still sleeping, but a steady stream of cars passed each other on the Golden Gate Bridge, commanding and mysterious, in a swirl of fog. So far above the picturesque scene, Warren felt a part of it yet removed, as though he was in his own world. That's how it had been last night, him and Charli in their own personal paradise.

So what happened? Obviously something. When he'd opened the shower door, it had shown in every fiber of her being. In the way she'd not turned around, the way he'd seen her shoulders tense. When it came to life and its circumstances, Warren handled things pretty analytically, in black-and-white. So when he thought about him and Charli he felt they either liked each other or they didn't; they wanted to be together or they would not. One thing for sure, what had happened between them was not something that could be pushed under the rug. They were going to have to talk about what happened last night, and what was happening now.

He listened. The water was still running. He walked to the bathroom. "Charli, I'm going to order room service. Would you like a traditional American breakfast with meat and eggs, or would you rather have pancakes, French toast or something light?"

"I'll have what you're having," was her response. "Except anything with tomatoes. I'm allergic."

With that, Warren was able to focus his thoughts on mundane things like ordering breakfast and sending their clothes out for an express cleaning. Then he picked up the newspaper that had been slid under the door, walked to the sitting area and sat to begin reading.

He opened the paper, turned the pages, but he didn't read a thing.

Figuring she couldn't hide in the bathroom forever and having washed and scrubbed and pondered and procrastinated until she was about to drive herself crazy, Charli finally turned off the shower, donned the bathrobe hanging on the back of the bathroom door and walked out into the room.

Warren looked up and began filling the air with sound. "Good morning. I ordered breakfast. Wasn't sure what to get you so I kind of ordered everything: eggs, bacon, hash browns, toast. Pancakes, fruit, orange juice and coffee. I also sent our clothes out so they can clean them.

"Oh, and I—"

"Drake."

"—called the company and they said the pilot—"

"Hey!"

He stopped.

"Slow your roll, cowboy." A quick almost-smile. "I agree with you."

Finally, Warren realized he'd been rambling. That he was nervous had not even occurred to him, since it rarely happened. "Agree with me about what?"

Charli walked over to the sitting area and sat on the edge of the chair facing him. "About what happened between our grandfathers years ago not being important now."

Warren sat silent, his brow slightly creased.

"I just had a come-to-Jesus meeting in the shower."

"You went to…Jesus?"

Charli's smile became genuine, as was her chuckle. "You've never heard that saying? It's where you come to terms with someone or something and resolve it. I've decided to resolve the negative, unwarranted feelings I've held for your family."

Looking out the window, she continued, "Everything I know about the Drakes, or thought I knew, came from my grandfather. For me, you guys were almost make-believe, like the people on TV. Heck, I even saw y'all on television and in the society pages of the *San Francisco Examiner* and the *Oakland Tribune.* No one I knew lived behind gilded gates, lounged in mansions or owned companies.

I'd see articles on your father and uncles, see pictures of your mother in the society pages and believe that what my grandfather said was true."

"Which was?"

"It's…not important."

"I'm just curious."

"Well…let's just say…the description would normally start with something bad and end with something worse."

"Ha!"

"I've always been blinded by my love for him, my un-equivocal devotion. But now I can see some of his anger for what it really was." She looked at Warren. "Jealousy."

"Your grandfather seemed to do well enough. That you still run the dairy farm he and my grandfather started is proof of that."

"It may look that way, but the truth of it is that things were very hard for my grandfather economically. Even now, finances remain precarious. My grandfather was a proud man, didn't like to ask for anything, didn't like for people to—" she used air quotes "—meddle in his af-fairs. And he didn't ever want me to believe that he was anything less than successful, unbeatable and amazing. I didn't find out about the financial shape of the farm until after he died. That's one of the reasons why I moved back to the farm. To help Griff. And to save what Grandpa and your grandfather started."

Warren listened intently, elbows on legs, fingers stee-pled beneath his chin. "I always assumed you grew up on the farm and had always lived there."

"I did grow up there, practically, and always was there a great deal of the summer. But remember, I told you that my parents lived in Oakland and that's where I grew up."

"Right."

"After college, I thought I'd outgrown the farm and stayed in Oakland, even though my parents had long since

moved away. But then my en—then things happened and…
my grandfather became ill and all of a sudden moving back
to the farm looked very appealing."

"What happened in Oakland?"

His voice was soft, caring. Charli had never talked much
about her failed engagement, had kept the hurt and shame
bottled up inside her, finding some comfort in working the
land. But now she realized these secrets made up part of
the hard shell around her heart. The heart that was yearning to know love again. The heart that wanted to experience it with Warren.

"During my freshman year of college, I met my first
true love. He was a junior, smart, charming, a great catch.
I felt lucky to be his girl. We dated throughout my college years and I was faithful, even though I began hearing rumors that for him that wasn't the case. Especially
after he graduated and began working in San Francisco's
financial district.

"But I loved him, had never loved another man. When
he asked me to marry him, I said yes."

After a long moment of silence, Warren prompted, "And
then…?"

Charli stood, went to the window and beheld a beautiful day, totally opposite the ugly memories that she now
relived. "Then he got another woman pregnant. A woman
I later found out he'd been seeing almost the entire time
we'd been together. High school sweethearts. He did the
right thing—"

Warren snorted.

Charli turned to him. "Right thing for *her,* and their
child. He married her. I was devastated. Ran back to the
farm to lick my wounds and heal." She walked back over
to the chair and plopped down. The journey down memory lane had been exhausting.

"What about Cedric?"

Charli tensed. "What about him?"

"I saw how you reacted that night at the dance. Something happened between you two. It's all right if you don't want to tell me what it was."

A knock provided Charli a reprieve. Warren went to the door, directed the waiter on where to place the cart and signed the check. He poured two glasses of orange juice and brought one to Charli. Neither made a move for the food.

She accepted the glass. "Thank you," she said, taking a thoughtful sip. "I've known Cedric from childhood and he's always been a pain. His uncle worked for my grandfather and Cedric would often accompany him to the farm, to harass me, mostly. One day, he cornered me in the barn and tried to assault me. If not for the fact that one of the stable hands walked in at that moment, I wouldn't have been a virgin when I met my ex-fiancé."

Chapter 28

She'd said that Charles Reed was proud. Warren could see that his granddaughter was just like him. The stories about Cedric and her ex had been delivered casually, but Warren could imagine how much courage it had taken her to share these hurtful memories. It warmed his heart, made him feel special that she trusted him enough to share them with him. It also made him want to makes sure that she never felt that kind of pain again.

"So what about you, Drake?" she said, her offhanded, sarcastic tone firmly back in place. She walked over to the food-bearing cart. "Since you're not married, you must have a sob story or two."

He joined her at the cart. They fixed their plates and walked over to the dining table. "I've had my share of heartbreak," he admitted as they began to eat. "But mine started at a much younger age."

Charli cocked a brow.

"Her name was Ramona, and I was all of nine."

"How old was she?"

"Sixteen."

Charli rolled her eyes. "Oh, please. No one loves at nine years old. That's infatuation."

"You couldn't have told me that. She was my nanny's daughter. Smelled like flowers, wore long braids like Janet Jackson did in *Poetic Justice and* could beat me at 'Mortal Kombat.' This chick was the business! I was in *love!*"

"Yeah, right." Her tone still held sarcasm but she was clearly enjoying the story.

"In high school and college," Warren continued, his tone changing. "That's when reality set in. People hear you have a little money and it changes things. I never knew whether a woman was after me for me or for what they thought they could get from me. I've had a couple girlfriends, but it never went as far as me presenting a ring."

"And you're not seeing anyone right now?"

He shook his head. "My last relationship ended about seven months ago, when I found out that she was using underhanded means to try to get pregnant."

"She told you she was on birth control and wasn't?"

"Worse. Needle holes in my condoms."

"No!"

"Yes."

"I don't believe it."

"I didn't want to. But it was true."

"Speaking of condoms…"

"I know, we didn't use them. I thought about that, too. I'm clean, though. Got tested right after I ended my last relationship, and again when I had my annual physical last month."

"I am, too," she said. "But…I'm not on the pill."

"Do you think you're pregnant?"

"God, I hope not!"

"Dang, Charli. Why'd you have to say it like that?"

"Do you want a baby?"

"Hell, no!"

They burst out laughing.

"Next time, we'll take the proper precautions."

"Oh, so you're sure there's going to be a next time, huh?"

"Only if you want it."

She reached over and grasped his hand. "I do."

Their conversation continued, easily gliding from one topic to another, until about thirty minutes later when the helicopter company called. Things moved quickly after that: their freshly dry-cleaned clothes arrived, then they were driven to the airport and an hour later descended on the makeshift landing spot outside Paradise Cove.

They walked to their cars and hugged.

"I guess it's time to get back to the real world," Charli said.

"Evidently," Warren said, checking his phone. "I've missed several calls, so something must be happening." He gave her a quick kiss. "See you tonight?"

"Sure."

A short time later, Warren turned from the highway onto the long, winding and now fully paved drive leading to his home. What he saw almost made him slam on the brakes. His house looked completely finished!

Maybe that's why he's been blowing up my phone, Warren thought, regarding the missed calls from Jackson. The calls from Walter and Ike, he felt, had to do with gold.

He parked his Maserati, walked around his beautiful, shingle-roofed home and back to the maze of deep holes that one day would be his pool area. As soon as he approached the group of men standing around an excavator, the questions and comments began.

"Boy, where have you been?"

"Mr. Drake, I have some questions."

"Warren! I've been calling you since yesterday!"

"Oh, so you finally decide to grace us with your presence? What's wrong with you?"

Against the barrage of comments and questions, he put up his hands in mock surrender. "Okay, okay. Look, I apologize for not returning your phone calls but what was supposed to be a few hours spent in San Francisco turned into an all-night affair."

Ike spoke first. "Sounds like you're about to go into your love life and, son, you can keep that to yourself."

"Speak for yourself," Walter grumbled. "I want to know about the filly who could take you away from the prospect of all this money!"

"And from the completion of your home," Jackson added.

"Is it finished?"

"Not totally. The men are still working on the inside. But it will be done by the weekend and ready for the interior designers to take over."

Warren reached out his hand to Jackson, "Thanks, man." He turned to Walter. "What's going on, Grandpa?"

"About a quarter million dollars' worth of gold, from the looks of things."

Warren's mouth dropped. "What?"

"Uh-huh, thought that would get your attention. Looks like we might have a good amount more if we keep tunneling west. Some of it looks to be on Reed property, so we'll need to pay them for the right to dig up their land and give them a small percentage of whatever is found on their land."

"Whoa, wait a minute. What are you saying?"

"We're the ones prospecting for the gold, son," Walter explained. "It's our investment, our machinery, our time and effort. So we'll pay them under a limited time lands right agreement and keep ourselves out of court."

"That's not how this is going to work. I've already spoken to Charli about it, and to my attorneys. She knows that there may be gold on their land. And while I didn't share this, I feel that whatever we find should be split fifty-fifty. That's how the papers were drawn up."

Walter frowned. "So we do all of the work and the Reeds still get half of the profit? How do you figure that?"

"Dad, I think I know how he figured it." Ike turned from Walter to Warren. "Is it Charli you spent the night with in San Francisco?"

"I thought you said you didn't want to hear about my love life."

Walter turned to Ike. "I have my answer." He turned to Warren. "Now, look. I can't fault you for getting a little poontang, but don't let it cloud your judgment, son."

"Charli isn't a piece of meat, Grandpa," Warren said, his voice rising along with his temper. "She's our neighbor and a landowner who needs to be treated with fairness and respect."

For a few seconds, nothing stirred but the wind.

"Perhaps we should discuss this later," Ike said.

"I don't think there's anything to discuss, Dad. Whatever gold we find will be split fifty-fifty."

"That may be how you feel about it, Warren," Ike replied. "But this land doesn't just belong to you. It belongs to the Drake family. So everyone should have a say in what happens."

"If I hadn't decided to make use of this land, start the vineyard and build this house, we wouldn't even be having this conversation. So I think that my feelings should be given *due* consideration. Grandpa, you and Charles Reed fell out over something that he deemed unfair." He held up his hand when Walter would have protested. "I'm not saying I believe it, even though I mostly only know your side of the story. So, sure, we can talk about it. But when it comes to this generation, specifically me and Charli, I want to turn the page on this feud by seeing whatever profits there are split right down the middle." He looked at his father, at Walter, at Jackson and at Tom. "And I mean that."

Chapter 29

Charli looked at the caller ID and took a deep breath. It was Alice, and Charli knew why she was calling: because a *staggering* amount of gold had been discovered on the Drake and Reed ranches. The scrutiny had been bad enough when it just a rumor. But that phrase—the media whore culprit's words, not Warren's or Charli's—had hit the news and now tongues were truly wagging all over town.

"Good morning, Miss Alice."

"Girl, is it true what I'm hearing?"

She could have asked what Alice was talking about, but that would have been wasted breath. "About the gold? Yes, it's true."

Alice squealed. "Ooh, Charlene. You're going to be rich!"

"Well, Miss Alice, I don't know about that."

"Charles always believed there was more gold on that

land than what he found. He's probably up in heaven doing a jig right about now."

The thought of her grandfather happy and dancing brought a smile to Charli's face.

"So how does that work, getting the gold, exchanging it for money and all?"

"What do you mean, exactly?"

"What do you think I mean? When are you going to get the cash so we can go shopping?"

"I don't know, Miss Alice. But however much it is, I don't plan on buying out any boutiques any time soon."

"Please don't tell me you're going to be a miser like your grandfather was. I was praying that when it came to clothes and shopping you'd inherited that gene from Cherise, not Charles."

"Ha!"

"Speaking of, have you told your mother?"

Charli frowned. "No, why would I do that?"

"Now, Charlene. I know that you and your mother aren't the best of friends, but Charles was her father. Her name is also on that land. She has a right to know."

"She never wanted anything to do with the farm! Left it as soon as she could and married my father."

"That may be, but right is right and wrong is wrong. Just remember that."

"What I'll remember is that she left Grandpa and me and ran away to Canada with her pseudorich new husband. I'll remember that she rarely calls me. I'll remember that when it's come to surviving since I was sixteen, Charles helped me, not Cherise. That's what I'll remember."

Alice's voice was low as she responded. "Okay. If you say so. But I also hope that you'll remember to do the right thing. The way Charles taught you. The way he would have wanted."

Charli took a deep, calming breath. "You're right, Miss

Alice. I will." A pause and then, "May I ask you something?"

"Sure, Charlene."

"Did Grandpa ever tell you what happened between him and Walter Drake?"

A slight hesitation and then, "Uh-huh."

"He told me that Walter stole from him, that they had a deal about the land and the business and Walter reneged on the deal."

"Well, baby, you know what they say. There are three sides to every story, those of the two parties involved... and the truth."

"Are you saying that that's not what happened?"

"I'm saying that Charles saw things from his perspective and had selective memory as the years went on."

"You sound pretty sure of what you're saying. Why's that?"

"Part of what I'm telling you is what he told me, and the other part I know because I was there."

"You were?" This information was news to Charli.

"You remember that I used to do the books for them when they first started their business?"

"Oh, right. I remember."

"The dairy always did good while Charles and Walter were partners. But after Walter left and returned to New Orleans, well, let's just say your grandfather wasn't always the best businessman."

"So Gramps lied to me all those years? Walter Drake wasn't responsible for his financial struggles, and the Drakes aren't as bad as he's made them out to be?"

Even as she said this she thought of Warren, and knew the answer.

Ashley sat in her mother's fancy hair salon—Joy's House of Style—getting a long, fresh weave. It was Friday, the place was crowded and as often happened when a bunch of women got together—gossip reigned.

"I heard that they were sleeping together," said one of the women, her hair sticking out all over with sections wrapped in foil.

"Who?" another asked, her ear sticking just far enough from under the dryer so as not to miss a word.

"The owner of Bucks and the new waitress."

Ashley rolled he eyes. "That little redhead with the big butt and the bigger ego, busing tables with an attitude and acting like she owns the place!"

Joy joined the others in laughter. "How can you think you're all that while taking somebody else's order and carrying dirty dishes?"

"Honey," Miss Foil responded, "Must be those tips she's getting after hours!"

Rachel, who'd had her hair washed, dried and conditioned and was now receiving a flatiron press, said nothing. But she was listening, hard, trying to miss neither consonant nor vowel.

"Speaking of tips," Under-the-Dryer continued. "Have y'all heard the latest? About the gold that the Drakes supposedly found on their property?"

Ashley perked up. Rachel leaned slightly toward the woman with the news.

"Read a little on the internet," Joy said, all ears as well. "Who'd you hear it from?"

The woman pulled her head from under the dryer. Dry hair would have to wait. "One of my girlfriends, whose boyfriend is working on the crew digging it up. Ooh, but I just remembered that I wasn't supposed to tell nobody so…y'all haven't heard this from me!"

The whole room burst into laughter.

"We're not going to say anything," Joy promised. "But is it really true? They've found gold?"

"They've got armed security walking the premises. What's that tell you?"

"It tells me that they're guarding something besides grapes."

"And not just the Drakes, but their neighbor, too."

"Who?" an older woman asked, putting down her magazine and looking at the woman under the dryer. "The Reeds? The ones who own that dairy farm?"

"I don't know their names," Under-the-Dryer said, slipping her head back under the hot air. "But I heard that they've dug up a lot of dirt on both properties, and nobody can just drive up and have a look. They've got it on lock!"

A new customer came back to where the women were sitting. Having heard the last bit of conversation, she joined in before her butt hit the chair. "What you guys are talking about is old news. The story ran in the *Chronicle* and is all over the internet. They even talked about it on our cable channel."

"Wow," Joy said with a sly glance at her daughter. "Those Drakes are money magnets!"

Rachel sat, contemplating what she'd just heard. A recent memory caused her to sit straight up.

"Don't move, Rachel. You're about to make me burn you with this iron!"

"Sorry."

Her eyes narrowed as she remembered the first of only a handful of conversations she'd had with Richard, and the one time they'd gone out. He was working for Warren, he'd told her, and had asked about gold. Then she remembered something else. The Paradise Ball and the woman who'd made Warren forget that Rachel was even in the room. Later she'd found out her name: Charlene Reed. *So...they're neighbors.* Now it made sense, why his quick text replies stated he was busy and why her phone calls had largely gone unreturned.

Rachel now knew what was going on. What she didn't know was what she'd do about it.

Later, when Joy had returned to the home that she and Ashley shared, she found her daughter and got right to the point. "What's going on with you and Niko?"

"Nothing. Why?"

"What do you mean, why? If I've taught you anything, I've taught you to go after the paper. You're beautiful, you're smart and you and Niko have been hanging out for a while. Why can't you get him to pop the question?"

"Niko's his own man, Mom. If I start pressuring him for a commitment that will simply push him away."

"Well, what about his younger brother, Terrell? Maybe he'd be an easier catch."

"Mom!"

"I know that sounds scandalous. But I'm just keeping it real. If one brother doesn't work, another one might. You'd better step up your game before somebody else does and ruins your chances of taking on the Drake name."

Two women, coming from two very different places, had a lot to think about.

Chapter 30

Richard sat at the bar in Acquired Taste, sipping Hennessy and Coke. It was his first day back in Paradise Cove since Warren had surprised him by giving him a week off, with pay, and he'd driven into Oakland on a whim and met a honey. He'd been holed up at her place for five days. Now he was back to pacify Rachel, whose phone calls he'd mostly dodged. They had a date tonight, but Richard knew he'd need to be fortified to put up with what he assumed would be an interrogation. Rachel was a pretty woman, the type of "good girl" his late mother would probably have liked to see him bring home. But the sister he'd met in Oakland was more his speed, and his taste. Like him, she liked to access her inner freak. So they had, with relish, all week long.

"Freshen that up for you?" the bartender asked.

"Why not?" Richard said.

"Can I get you something to snack on?"

"No, thanks, man. I'm going to dinner in a little bit."

"And that won't be here?" The bartender put both hands over his heart. "Say it isn't so!"

"This is my favorite place, you know that. But everybody has to switch it up every now and then."

The bartender smiled and nodded as he wiped down the counter. "I hear you." He looked up as another man sat down. "Cedric! My man!" He walked over and gave the man a fist pound.

"Hey, Duane."

"The usual?"

Richard watched as Cedric answered, then looked over and nodded in greeting. Richard nodded back.

"Don't I know you?" Cedric asked.

"I don't think so."

"You work over there with Warren, right?"

Richard scowled. The brother had just sat down and was already asking too many questions. "I might. Why?"

"Sorry, man, I don't mean to pry." He moved and sat so there was only one bar stool between them. "Cedric Martin." He held out his hand. "I'm good friends with his neighbor, Charli Reed."

This got Richard's attention. "Richard Cunningham."

The men shook hands. The bartender delivered Cedric's drink. "Oh, and hook me up with an order of those gourmet hot wings," Cedric said.

"Coming right up."

"Yeah," Cedric continued once the bartender had gone to the other end of the counter. "It's crazy what's happening over there with Charli."

"What's going on?"

"You haven't heard? They found a bunch of gold over on both her and Warren's property."

Richard sat back, his eyes narrowed. "You don't say."

"Yeah, man. Heard the brother was having a hole dug for his swimming pool and struck gold! I guess instead of

water, him and Charli are going to be swimming in cash!"
He laughed at his own joke and took a big swig of liquor.

Richard's smile was easy but inside his blood boiled.
Now it all made sense: the men leaving early after that
first hole was dug, the area being cordoned off shortly
thereafter. When he'd asked, Jackson had said it was for
safety reasons. *Yeah, it was safety, all right. The safety of
Warren's riches!*

"I didn't even know that that still happened, people
finding gold," Richard said.

"Yes, it does, and that's not even the first time."

"Oh, yeah?"

Cedric told Richard the other story that had resurfaced,
about Charles Reed and Walter Drake's find all those years
ago. "Some people are just lucky, I guess," he finished. "I'd
give anything to get my hands on that gold!"

"You should ask your girl to let you help mine it. You
said that Charli's your friend, right?"

"We grew up together, but…I don't know that we're
tight enough for her to trust me like that."

"Guess trust is hard to come by."

"Meaning?"

"I was one of the men working on Warren's house."

"Oh, so you already know about the gold."

"Not until now. Interestingly enough, I was given an
unscheduled vacation last week." Richard gave Cedric a
look. "Guess the timing wasn't coincidental."

"Sounds like he trusts you about as much as Charli
does me."

"I guess. But like you, I'd do anything to get my hands
on that gold."

"You might have a chance if you could get past the security guarding Warren's office building."

Richard leaned forward. "I'm listening."

"Heard some of the gold is stored in a room there before it's picked up and hauled away to parts unknown."

"Do you know how it's transported?"

Cedric shrugged. "Nobody's sure about that. On any given day there are a flurry of vans, pickups, you name it coming and going from the property. I suspect it's precisely so no one can figure out who's carrying the goods."

"A sure carjacking if someone found out."

"You know it. A gold jacking, more like it!"

The men paused as the bartender brought over Cedric's hot wings. "I'll get you a glass of ice water to go with those," he chuckled.

"Make that two," Richard said.

"You got it. Still don't want anything to eat?"

"Naw, man. I'm good." After he walked away, Richard took a sip of his drink. "I wonder how many men he has guarding the stash."

Cedric gave Richard a side-eyed glance. "Why? You thinking about trying to lighten Warren and Charli's load a little bit?"

Richard looked at Cedric. "Are you?"

"Hell, yes," Cedric replied, as his brows creased. "I've got a score to settle with little Miss Charli."

"Sounds like there's some history between you two."

"My uncle used to work on Charli's farm and I spent a lot of time there," Cedric replied. "I know that property like the back of my hand, pretty much. Different ways you can get in." He paused, then added, "Without being seen." He finished his drink and set the glass on the bar counter a little harder than necessary. "Even though they've got guards posted and whatnot." His laugh was sinister. "I know how to get through."

"You need some help?" Richard asked.

Cedric picked up a wing. "You volunteering?"

"Hell, yeah. As long as we can split the spoils."

The bartender brought over the glasses of ice water and both men ordered another drink. Richard called Rachel and told her that he'd be late picking her up. The men put their heads together, voices low, and continued to plot and plan. Richard justified his upcoming actions by thinking Warren should have told him about the gold and cut him in, their being old friends and whatnot. Cedric's motive was more obvious—he didn't get the girl.

Payback was a bitch, both men agreed. They also felt that for them…payday was coming.

Chapter 31

"I thought I'd made myself quite clear on this," Charli said, pushing an errant curl back under her cowboy hat. They were standing in the driveway, admiring Warren's newly landscaped front yard. "I won't accept your offer."

It was the day after Warren had had the tense conversation with his father and grandfather, and later the family, about the Reed Ranch and how to handle the distribution of profit from the gold. After that, he'd called his attorneys and given the green light for the final draft of the contract to be executed and sent over for Charli's signature. Obviously, she'd read it.

"I'm sorry if I phrased that like a question. It was a statement. The profits will be split fifty-fifty." His voice became stern, authoritative. "It's a decision I've made, one not up for discussion."

He watched as her jaw clenched and her nostrils flared. *Damn, you're sexy when you're angry.* He crossed his arms and held his ground.

"You've made all the investment, for machinery and manpower."

"True."

"Even after deducting those expenses, a sixty-forty split would be more than generous."

"The split will be fifty-fifty of the gross profits."

"We've got to—"

"Don't argue with me, woman."

"Don't push me, Drake."

"The name's Warren." The air crackled with tension as Warren watched Charli war with her emotions. When he saw her shoulders relax, a smile slowly stretched across his face. "A simple thank-you will suffice."

Her eyes narrowed. She tucked her hands into her back pockets. "I don't like this, Drake. Fair is fair."

"You're welcome."

She let out an exasperated breath. "Fine. Thank you."

"Thank you, *Warren*."

"You really are pushing it." He lifted a brow. "Warren. Thanks."

His heart warmed at the sound of his name on her tongue. He liked the way her lips pursed as she said it, and how her arms behind her brought attention to those round, brown breasts that he loved so much.

Which reminded him of the other reason why he'd asked her to come over. "The house is finished."

"Already?"

"I had them put a rush on it—wanted to be in there during as much of the harvest as possible."

"I've wondered about how that works, having a vineyard and all."

"It's already begun, but we still have two good months of harvest left, so I'd be happy to show you around, tell you as much about it as I know. In fact my cousin Dexter, the true expert, is due back soon. I'll have you over for dinner, let him guide the tour. It's pretty exciting, actually."

"Sounds interesting. I'd like that. How do you like your new home?"

"It's beautiful. Kind of empty, though." Her expression was unreadable. "I'm going to spend the night here tonight, for the first time. I'd love it if you'd join me. I'm even going to try my hand at cooking a meal."

"And you want me to be the guinea pig?"

"Who'd you think would be cooking when you came for dinner with Dexter?"

Charli shrugged. "I thought bourgie possums like you had chefs." Her eyes twinkled as she repeated the term she'd eventually shared with him in San Francisco, a favorite of her grandfather's when it came to the Drakes.

Warren smirked as he stepped closer and wrapped his arms around her. "I promise not to poison you. But I can't say the same for whether or not the steak will be over- or undercooked."

"Steak, you say? Don't bother with the experiment. Both in the field and in the kitchen, the cow is my forte. What time do you want dinner?"

He looked at his watch. "Does seven-thirty work for you?" She nodded. "Okay, I'll be back soon."

About a half a mile away, on the other side of the two-lane highway in front of the Reeds', Cedric lay in the ditch, a pair of binoculars up to his eyes. They were pinned on Charli and Warren. Talking about something serious, Cedric assumed, if Charli's face was any indication. But then she said something, and Warren laughed before wrapping his arms around her. Cedric frowned. Something about the way she looked up at Warren made the vein in his neck throb. For years he'd chased her and wished that she would look at him that way.

"That's all right, witch," he muttered, adjusting the binoculars as his subjects began to come closer, Warren walking Charli to her car. "Before this week is over the only thing you and that asshole will have to hold on to is this wretched country land, those stinky-ass cows…and each other."

"What are you doing?" Griff asked, watching as Charli pulled ears of corn, potatoes and a few spices from the pantry. "I've already cooked beans, corn bread and baked chicken. It's almost ready."

"I'm heading back out," Charli replied, knowing that the answer wouldn't be enough information but deciding to answer only to what was asked.

"Where?"

"Over to the Drake place." Purposely, she didn't meet his eyes but rather pulled one of the recycle bags out of the drawer and placed the vegetables inside it. Then she went back into the pantry for oil and flour.

"As a cook?"

"As a neighbor. Drake's house is finished."

"And he don't have food?"

After scouring the shelves, she went to the freezer for a package of rolls. "I don't know. But I thought it would be nice to fix him a meal."

She picked up the bag and prepared to leave. Griff stopped her. "I don't like it. Now, don't get me wrong. He seems like a nice enough fella, especially for a Drake. But your grandfather would—"

"Griff, I've always respected you, felt your words had the same kind of weight that Grandpa's did. And I know about the bad blood between him and Walter Drake. But it's his bad blood, Griff. Not mine. You're right. Drake is a good man. We've become good friends."

"How good?"

In a rare show of affection between them, Charli kissed her play uncle's grizzled cheek. "Goodbye, Griff."

"I'll wait up for you."

She stopped in the doorway, turned and answered, "Don't."

Five minutes later, Charli pulled up to Warren's beautifully landscaped, warmly lit house, and sat, amazed. Anyone who didn't know otherwise would have thought the home had been there forever. There was not a speck of remaining dust from the construction, not a blade of the new grass out of place. Flowers danced with the wind, a lit water feature gurgled melodically and the arrangement of shrubs and bushes bordered by large colored stones looked to have come straight out of an architectural magazine. Charli was reminded of the vast difference between them when it came to money and for a moment, she felt out of place. She looked at the recycle bag from the grocery store, her simple blue tank top—clean but old—well-worn jeans and sandals. Looking at his house she felt as though she should be wearing satin and pearls.

Any thoughts that she might have had to cut and run were abolished when she looked up and saw Warren at the front door. He looked as casual as she, wearing a pair of khaki shorts that looked as though they'd seen better days, a beige polo shirt, leather sandals and a welcoming smile. She grabbed the bag of food, took a deep breath and exited the car.

"Howdy, partner!" Warren walked toward where her truck was parked.

It was dorky, but just the greeting she needed to calm her nerves.

"Drake," she replied, stepping into his open arms for a brief hug. He reached for the bags that she was carrying before they went inside.

* * *

A short distance away, Cedric and Richard sat in a borrowed car, a nondescript Honda that could be found on any highway. Cedric had borrowed it from a friend as neither man wanted their rather showy vehicles—Cedric's BMW or Richard's classic Cadillac—anywhere around the soon-to-be crime scene.

Richard looked at Cedric after watching Warren and Charli enter the house. "Looks like your girl has a new friend."

Cedric made a sound of disgust. "Man, he can have my leftovers."

"Oh, you've already hit that?"

"Please. I sampled that piece of country from one side of the ranch to the other. Every time my uncle went to work for her grandpa, I went to work on her."

"Hey, with a history like that, I'm surprised you're not still friends."

"I got tired of her and kicked her to the curb. She never got over it. Hates me to this day for breaking her heart."

"It sounds like your stealing the gold is a bit of a vendetta."

Cedric shook his head. "Not at all. This isn't personal, Richard. This is business."

"I feel the same way." Richard looked toward the house. "We know where two people on the property are. And we know that they'll be busy. So all we need to do is locate all of the security detail and take out the guy guarding the office door."

"Piece of cake," Cedric snarled as he put on a cap and dark glasses.

While Cedric used the disposable phone he'd just purchased to call their accomplices, Richard turned the vehicle onto what used to be a car lane but was now overgrown with weeds. He pulled forward until the car was no longer visible from the road.

Then he turned off the car and turned to Cedric. "Are you ready?"

"Born so."

"Cool. Let's do this."

Chapter 32

"Oh my God! Will you marry me?" Warren had just taken his first bite of Charli's home-cooked meal.

"No," she replied with a giggle and a smile of appreciation at his remark. "I refuse to accept a proposal delivered around a mouthful of food!"

They bantered lightly. Warren continued to rant and rave about the perfectly cooked medium-rare steak, creamy whipped potatoes, fried corn, rolls and a trio of roasted vegetables, carrots, turnips and brussels sprouts.

After a light dessert of vanilla-bean ice cream, Warren and Charli made quick work of cleaning up the kitchen before settling into Warren's smartly decorated living room. It was a skillful blend of opulence and comfort, in soothing shades of cream, tan and brown with splashes of primary accent colors in pillows, vases and art.

"I know I said it before, but I really love your place. I know that everything in here is new and expensive, but it doesn't feel stuffy and cold." She gave the room one more look before turning to Warren. "It fits you."

He leaned over and kissed her. "Thanks." It was so nice, he did it twice. "Umm. I've missed you."

Charli hid her nervousness behind a teasing tone. "You see me every day."

He ran his finger over her thin top, ran his thumb back and forth across her nipple and watched it quickly come to life. "I've missed what I can't see."

His touch made her body thrum and turned the shy girl bold. "I've seen your downstairs. Why don't you show me what is—" she nodded toward the staircase "—up there."

Warren simply smiled, stood, took her hand and led the way.

Outside, two men dressed in black from head to toe slowly crept toward the building that housed Warren's office. They came from the back, making use of the cover that the trees and vines laden with grapes and leaves provided, crouching behind them before using a collapsible ladder to easily scale the six-foot fence. Cedric was the first man over with Richard right behind him. Within minutes, two other men joined them near a gate that Cedric unlocked. The four men crept along a rarely used back road toward the cordoned-off area protected by security guards, near where the mine shaft helped to keep them hidden. Using a mound of dirt both for cover and leverage, they crawled up far enough to see without being seen and tweaked their game plan.

"Okay, y'all can see that there's one dude over there," Cedric whispered as he pointed to where a man lounged near the temporary fence surrounding the holes, the fence that the men had penetrated from behind. "And another dude is patrolling the perimeter. It takes him about ten minutes to walk the whole thing, fifteen if he stops and smokes a cigarette and talks on the phone like he usually does. There's another guard normally keeping the front locked down. He hangs near the driveway mostly. And then there's the joker guarding the office door. JT, I want you to stay and keep an eye on these two fools. All right?" JT nodded. "You see anything out of the ordinary, or one of them heading toward where we are, send me a quick text like we planned.

"When we get by the office, I'll keep watch on the guard by the drive. Sam, you handle the guard by the office door and, Richard, you need to work that lock as quickly as you can."

"Man, don't talk like you're schooling me," Richard said through clenched teeth. "This isn't my first time on the wrong side of the law."

"Maybe, but when was the last time your ass stole some gold?"

"Stealing is stealing, it don't matter the product. I'm not a rookie, son. Back up off me."

The third guy, Sam, interrupted their little power play. "Look, y'all, we don't have time for this! We've got a job to do."

Richard and Cedric glared at each other for another second before Cedric continued. "Sam, I want you to go first, a little ahead of me and Richard, handle that guard and send the signal. Are you sure you can take him?"

Sam flexed his bulging biceps. "Man, I'm going to knock that fool smooth out."

"Soon as the coast is clear, send that text. Me and Richard will be waiting by the stables to scoop up the goods while you continue to keep watch outside. Everybody cool on their assignment?"

The men all nodded. "Good," Cedric said. Anybody have any problems, hit me up on the cell right away. Anything go down, somebody gets noticed, we all pull out and meet up later at the spot." He looked each man in the eye. "All right, then. Let's go get this money."

Cedric crouched down and watched Sam's stealthy movements as he crept beyond the outer edge of the area where they knew motion lights were placed. He knew that his homeboy would go counterclockwise to the guard's movements, placing himself next to the office when the guard most likely to cause problems—other than the one at the door—would be the farthest away. Once a minute or so had passed, Richard and Cedric followed a similar path to the one Sam had taken, except instead of heading straight to the office they crept toward the stables. While Richard did a quick check to make sure no two-legged animal was on their side of the building, Cedric positioned himself under the stable's overhang, totally hidden against the outer wall. While waiting for Sam's signal he took a deep breath. For now he was safe; no eyes were on him.

None, that is, except that of the long-range camera attached to the stable roof, outfitted with spy-vision night scope and aimed squarely at where he was hiding.

Less than five minutes passed before Cedric's phone lit up beneath his shirt. The guard had been immobilized. He stood and joined Richard, who'd remained near the edge of the building, watching for movement. Silently, quickly, they covered the distance between the stables and the office. Having honed his skills while serving time, Richard went to work on the office door locks and within seconds they were in.

"This house is stunning."

"I'm glad you like it." Warren had finished the upstairs tour and now he and Charli were cuddled in his king-size bed.

She reached between them and massaged his dick. "This is pretty stunning, too."

"Hmm, you think so?"

"Yes," she said, sitting up and throwing back the covers.

"What are you doing?"

"Judging beef is my business, you know." She continued talking casually as she straddled him, as if they were discussing her latest livestock buy. The only hint of her devilishness was her saucy demeanor as she looked at him, and the way she tossed her hair away from her eyes. For a moment she simply stared, took time to appreciate this magnificent, toned specimen, his dark skin highlighted against stark white sheets. "I have an eye for good color and yours is…" She gave his hardening manhood a squeeze. "Spectacular."

Of course…one good squeeze deserved another.

"Another quality one looks for is nice muscle." Sliding her hand up and down the length of him, she cooed, "This piece right here is thick—" she bounced his shaft against her hand a couple times "—weighty." And then alternated between pulling and squeezing. His sex became as hard as steel. She cocked a brow. "And firm."

Her clinical analysis of his body was driving him crazy. When she scraped a nail across his mushroom tip, he almost whimpered.

"Of course," she continued, "the final and most important test of any good grade of beef is…" She became silent, smiling, rubbing his dick as she looked at him.

"Is what?" The question came out in a hoarse tone.

"The taste." She wet her lips, lowered her head and took the tip of him into her mouth.

He hissed and from the corner of her eye she saw his hands grab the sheets.

She raised up her head. "You okay?"

"Perfect," he eked out between gritted teeth.

The taste test continued. "Did I tell you that I love mushrooms?"

His head moved from side to side. For the life of him, he couldn't speak. Not a word.

"Well, I do." She outlined the perfect mushroom at the tip of his penis with her fingernail before repeating the process with her tongue. "Very nice." Once again, she took him into her mouth, the assault shifting between tongue and tugs, nails and nips, while fondling his delightfully soft sac.

"Baby, I—I—I can't take it…"

She chuckled, the throaty, knowing laugh of a woman fully in control. "Then let's go to part two of this inspection." She lifted up and poised herself over him. "Oh, yes," she breathed, settling slowly down on his rock-hard cock. "This is an amazing—" she slid up "—grade A—" she slid back down "—prime—" she gyrated her hips and he joined her "—piece of meat."

"You know," he panted, meeting her stroke for stroke. "That as soon as we finish with this part of your inspection…I'm going to do mine."

"I'm counting on it, cowboy."

He squeezed her juicy butt cheeks, grabbed her hips and helped her get to know every single inch of his prime grade-A beef.

Chapter 33

Warren's ringing cell phone woke him out of a deep slee
He'd first awakened a couple hours before, when Char
had insisted on slipping out of the house around 2:00 a.r
He looked at the clock. It was seven-thirty.

"Yes." He answered the call and put it on speaker, h
voice gruff as his head hit the pillow and he closed h
eyes.

"Sorry to wake you, Warren, but we've got a problen
Warren's eyes flew open. "What kind of problem?"
"A break-in."
He rolled out of bed in an instant. "Where?"
"The office building."
"I'll be right there."
Less than ten minutes later Warren, wearing a T-shi
sweats and slip-on sandals, reached his office. Standi
just outside the door was Johnny, the head of Warren's s
curity detail, and another of the guards on duty last nig

"Where's Dennis?" Warren asked.

"He's at the hospital. He's okay," Johnny hurriedly dded. "Took a pretty hard knock upside the head and has concussion. But he'll be released by the end of the day."

Warren turned toward the office door.

"Don't touch anything," Johnny warned. "We don't want to mess up fingerprints, fibers, DNA or any other ype of evidence." Johnny used a paper towel to push the oor wider so that they could enter. "They got into your ffice," he continued, over his shoulder. "Obviously they ere looking for the gold that's kept here."

"Did they find it?" Warren asked, able to deliver a slight mirk despite the circumstances.

"You know what the security room is made of," Johnny nswered, smiling himself. "Not even the heaviest door m could penetrate that many inches of steel. There are cratches around the lock where the thief obviously made valiant effort at trying to get in. No such luck."

They'd reached Warren's office. He looked around. For-nately when it came to his professional domain, he liked minimalist look. Most of the books had been pulled from e shelves, and his file cabinet had been broken into. They took my golf clubs," he noted, looking at the now-re corner.

Johnny noted pieces of broken porcelain behind the sk.

Warren followed his line of vision. "There were a few old nuggets in that jar, worth about fifty cents, maybe dollar."

"Anything else missing that you can think of?"

"No." Warren continued to look around. "Oh, wait. I d have two fairly large chunks of gold sitting on that ookshelf. So I guess they got me for, oh, a few hundred aybe."

Johnny gave Warren a sympathetic pat on the back as passed him. "I guess I'll go and look around the place,

check the stables, the horses. Maybe it wasn't someone
after the gold. Maybe it was just some kids trying to van
dalize—saw there was nothing here and moved on. But
guess we should get the police out here and make a report

Warren turned to look at him. "Do you really believ
that?"

"Not for a second. Just don't want to have you worry
ing, boss. We'll get to the bottom of this."

"Johnny, you are absolutely right."

Charli was humming a tune by Adele as she sat astrid
Butterscotch looking at the cattle. She'd led a group c
them to the stream while Griff was at the house helping th
men there to fix the roof. Bobby and the other men wer
busy doing their various chores. It was a typical yet beau
tiful September morning, one even more special to Chau
because of how she'd spent a good part of last night—
Warren's arms.

Her phone vibrated against her side. She pulled it o
of its holder and as if she conjured him up, saw his nan
on her screen. "Hey there, cowboy."

"Hello, Charli."

There was no sexy in his voice. "What's wrong?"

"We had a break-in last night."

"A break-in? Are you serious?"

"Unfortunately, yes. Someone found out or figured o
that a small amount of the gold is sometimes kept here,
the office building. They tried to get it."

"Were they successful?"

"No."

He sigh was audible. "Good."

"I take it that nothing is out of place over there? Not
ing's missing?"

"Not that any of us has noticed. Hold on a momen
She placed the call on hold, whistled for Bobby who w

nearby. "I'm going over to the Drake place," she told him, then turned her horse in that direction.

"I'm back, Drake. So they didn't take anything?"

"They broke into my office. Took my golf clubs, those tiny nuggets I showed you and a couple larger chunks that were sitting on my shelf. That's about it. Can you come over here?"

"I'm already on my way."

By the time Charli got there, the police had also arrived. One officer looked around while another took the report.

"We have security cameras," Warren said to the officer beside him, after detailing the other information.

The officer's head shot up. "Well, let's have a look."

Warren, Charli, Johnny and the officer squeezed inside the room the thieves hadn't bothered with but probably could have gotten into, the room filled with screens from six security cameras and holding expensive photography and video equipment.

"This obviously wasn't a random robbery," the officer said with a quick look around. "They only broke into your office, and missed all of the valuables in here."

A look passed between Johnny, Charli and Warren. These three knew exactly what the thieves had wanted.

The group huddled around the screens and after designating a person to view each one, with Warren and Johnny each looking at two, they began the tedious process of going through footage.

"We can adjust the speed so that it fast-forwards," Warren said, turning a series of knobs. The pictures were a bit grainy but the night-vision cameras had lived up to their price tag. And after about ninety minutes of searching the previous night's footage, shadows appeared on screen number four.

"I think I have something!" Charli shouted.

Warren paused the tapes and rewound the one for screen four. "That's the one over the stable," he muttered.

Four heads moved as one toward the screen.

"I think I see two figures," the officer said. "One crouched, and the other standing near the edge of the building." He pointed toward the figures.

"Too dark to make them out, though," Johnny said with a sigh.

They watched. Waited. Soon, the two men by the barn crept closer to the camera as they headed toward the office building. As the lead man stepped from beneath the overhang, his face was lightened by the light of the moon. Illuminated just enough to enhance his facial features.

As one, four heads moved closer to the screen.

"Any idea who it is?" the officer asked.

Warren shook his head, squinting as he looked. "Wait I can isolate a part of the screen and blow it up. Hold on." He messed with a few more knobs. "Dang, I haven' played around with this board too much. Oh, here it is Here we go."

He moved a rectangle over the area where the man sat cropped the picture and then, using another knob, began to increase the picture's size. As it did, the face became clearer.

"I still can't tell..." Warren's words died as he tried to recognize the subject.

"I can."

Three pairs of eyes looked at Charli.

She looked at Warren. "It's Cedric."

Warren frowned. "Are you sure?"

Johnny asked, "Who's Cedric?"

"Ma'am, do you think you can make a positive ID?" the officer queried.

Charli crossed her arms and looked at the officer. "I am positive that the man in this picture is an old acquaintanc of mine. He's a local and knows this area very well. His name is Cedric. Cedric Martin."

"You're sure about this?" the officer asked.

Charli gave her signature curt nod. "Positive."

Chapter 34

Warren and Charli stood in his driveway as the police cars drove away. He put a protective hand on her shoulder as they watched the cars until they were barely visible.

Charli turned into Warren's chest. "This is crazy. Cedric is a lot of things but I didn't count thief among them."

"Any man who will assault a woman is capable of the lowest of crimes."

She looked up at him. "What will you do now?"

"What the officers said, increase the number of men on security, install more lights, cameras and a more advanced security system." He felt her shiver. "Don't worry, baby. The police know at least one person responsible and after they lock him up, I'm sure this little problem will go away."

She stepped away from him and looked around. "I don't even have the money yet and already it's causing me problems."

"Is that what you think? That having money isn't a good thing?"

"I didn't say 'not good.' I said 'problematic,' and I won't take that back."

"There are more things to worry about, more responsibility, when you have wealth. But the benefits heavily outweigh the disadvantages."

"If you say so." Charli felt her phone vibrate. "Hold on." She touched the screen. "Hello?" A frown immediately appeared on her face. "Why, what's wrong?" She listened for a few moments. "How did that happen?" She was already running to her car as she concluded, "I'll be right there."

Warren rushed to catch up with her. "Charli! What's going on?"

Her eyes were wild with worry. "It's Griff. He's taken a fall. It's serious. I've got to go."

Charli jumped in her truck and flew down the highway. In minutes, she was jumping out of it and running toward the house.

Bobby came from around the side of the house. "Charli! He's back here!"

She jumped off the porch and ran around to the back of the house, on Bobby's heels. As soon as they turned the corner she saw him: sprawled out on the ground, mouth tight, fists clenched, in obvious pain. She ran and dropped down beside him. Placing a shaky hand on his shoulder, she took a breath and said, "I know you didn't want me at the Drake place, but isn't this attempt of getting me to come back a bit dramatic?"

He shook his head and groaned. Not quite the reaction she was expecting. This might be worse than she thought. "Can you talk, Griff? Tell me where you're hurting."

"Leg," he ground out between clenched teeth.

"Just lie there and don't move, okay? The ambulance is on its way."

"Drink."

"Bobby, go pour a shot of Griff's whiskey and bring it here."

One of the workers commented, "Charli, I don't think we should—"

"Shut up!" She turned to Bobby. "Do it. Now!"

Bobby raced to the back door and quickly returned with a full shot of the clear liquid. Charli eased Griff's head up just enough to rest on her knees. Then she slowly placed the glass to the old man's lips. He drank down the liquid and sighed. "Another."

She gave the glass to Bobby, who raced back in the house, throwing a warning glance in the direction of the worker who'd earlier commented. The newbie averted his eyes. By the time Bobby arrived with the second shot of liquor, they could hear the blare of the ambulance siren in the distance.

"Hear that, Griff? Help is almost here. Hang in there, Uncle. You're going to be fine."

Three hours later, a weary yet relieved Charli neared the city limits of Paradise Cove, having left Griff at the nearest hospital, almost thirty miles away. She hated the thought of him being injured but was thankful that he'll live. Remembering that she'd earlier seen a missed call from Warren, she called him.

"Drake, it's me."

"I've been worried about you, baby. How's Griff?"

"His leg is busted up pretty good and he sustained a bruised wrist when he tried to break the fall, but otherwise he's all right."

"What happened?"

"He was up on the roof."

"Oh, no."

"Yep. Being hardheaded. The men tried to talk him out of helping, but Griff has a hard time seeing other people working and not joining in. It's just his nature. Some how his foot got tangled in a rung and he took a fall off the ladder."

"How long is he going to be in the hospital?"

"The doctor said four to five days, but I doubt they'll be able to keep him that long. I doubt that Griff has slept more than six hours or lain in a bed longer than eight at time in twenty-five, thirty years. But they've got some ute nurses. That might provide some incentive."

"There you go." A pause and then, "How are *you* oing?"

"I was pretty shook up a while ago, but I'm better now. eeing him lying there, it hit me just how much he means o me. Next to Grandpa, I'm closest to Griff. If anything appened to him I couldn't handle it. After patching him p, they gave him a sleeping pill. Said that he'd be knocked ut until morning."

"I read somewhere that sleep is a healer. He'll be back his old self in no time."

"Hopefully you're right."

"Of course I'm right. I'm always right."

"Cool it, Drake."

He laughed. "Listen, why don't you come over, spend e night? We'll take a nice, long bubble bath. And you can ok me dinner again. I could get used to that."

"That sounds really tempting, but I think I should stay the house tonight. There are chores to be done and one the heifers is close to birthing. I'll call you later, when n lying in bed. Naked. Wet. Thinking about you."

"Girl, quit playing."

"Ha! See you later."

"Bye."

There was so much work to be done that the day passed ickly, ending with Charli making the boys a large pot of ef stew. She rounded it out with a golden pan of corn-

bread and, because she wasn't the baker that Griff was
threw together a simple batch of oatmeal cookies.

The men were much obliged.

Aside from Charli telling them about the break-in, an
encouraging them all to be more alert, the dinner conversation was quiet. Everyone worried about Griff.

When they finished, Bobby turned to her. "Do you wan
me to stay here, Charli? I can bunk on the couch."

"Thanks, Bobby, but that won't be necessary. I'll b
fine."

"You sure?"

"Positive."

The men left and after washing up the dishes, Char
settled on the couch. She watched television for about a
hour and then began to yawn, her body finally aware c
the long, full day that had followed her long, love-fille
night. "Lucy?" She looked around for her big, fat feline
"Lucy, where are you?" It just now came to her that sh
hadn't seen the cat all day, not even in the stables, when
she usually hung out. "Oh, well," she mumbled, getting o
the couch and heading toward her bedroom. "It's not th
first time you've spent the night under the stars."

She took a shower and pulled on a pair of her favori
pajamas. Then she padded into the kitchen, barefoot, f
a couple cookies and a glass of milk.

Yeow!

Charli froze, her hand in midreach. Her heart beat
a rapid pace.

Meow.

"Oh, my goodness." She placed a hand over her hea
and took deep breaths. "That's the cat."

She walked over and opened the back door. "Luc
Come on, girl." She looked the length of the porch. *Whe
is she?*

"Lucy!" *You frustrating feline!* Frustrated herse

Charli stomped into the house to put on shoes so that she could go out into the yard. She slipped on her leather sandals, grabbed a flashlight and turned to see Cedric standing in her doorway. He held her cat in one hand, a gun in the other.

He leaned against the doorjamb, stroking the cat's fur with the gun. "Finally, we're both after the same thing. A little pussy."

Chapter 35

Warren walked the twins to the door. Aside from discuss ing the break-in, their unexpected visit had given him an evening filled with jokes and laughter. And it hadn't hur that they'd bought him a pan of lasagna and a containe of salad, compliments of his parents' chef.

"All right, y'all. Take it easy."

"You too, man." Terrell and Warren shared a handshak and a shoulder bump.

Warren leaned down to hug Teresa. "Thanks for think ing about me and bringing me dinner."

"Not that you couldn't stand to lose a few pounds…"

"Excuse me?"

"But we didn't want you to starve."

"Okay, get out of here!" Warren gave her a playful shov and then followed them out onto the porch. "Tell the folk I'll be over there tomorrow."

"Will do!" Teresa said, and waved.

The two got into Terrell's car and drove away. Warre

watched them until their car left the driveway, then looked around and spotted Johnny, his head guard. He threw up a hand to him also before walking back inside.

Looking at his watch, he was surprised to see that it was almost ten o'clock. And he hadn't heard from Charli. He walked to his master suite, deciding to take off his clothes and get comfortable before giving her a call.

"Cedric, if you just leave right now, we can forget all about this." Charli worked to undo the rope that held her hands behind her back.

"Shut up! I'm in control now." He paced the room, waving the gun. "I say what happens! After what you did to me, you'd better hope it's not fatal."

Charli swallowed her fear. She had to remain calm. Her life depended on it. "Cedric," she said, her voice soft and low. "What is it that I did to you?"

"You had me locked up!"

"How could I have done that? I didn't even know you were in jail!" Earlier, when he'd talked about the break-in at Warren's place, she'd said she didn't know about it, had told him that when she left his house Warren was asleep and that they hadn't talked since because of Griff's accident. It was a logical explanation. Unfortunately Cedric was an illogical man.

"If you didn't do it, your man did. So whether it's him directly or you by default, you're still going to feel pain. And then he'll get what's coming to him, too!"

Her phone rang. She held her breath. Cedric walked over and snatched it off the table. "Well, well, well. Speak of the devil."

"I—I—I'd better answer it, Cedric. Or he'll think something's wrong."

Cedric hesitated, his eyes darting back and forth as he considered what she said.

The phone stopped ringing.

Charli's heart dropped. Warren was her only chance unless she could get loose and get to one of her weapons. *Damn!*

Cedric stomped over and knelt down beside her. Charli tensed, forcing herself to breathe evenly as he ran a jagged fingernail over her cheek. "Okay, sweetheart, listen carefully because I'm only going to say this once. I'm going to call your boy back and you're going to let him know that everything over here is fine and that you don't want him over here. I'm going to put it on speaker so that I can hear everything." He put his finger under her chin and forced her to look up. "Try anything and things will get real ugly. Got it?"

"Okay, except…"

"Except what? C'mon, tramp, spit it out!"

"Warren hates it when I talk on speaker."

"Well I'm *not* going to let you talk where I can't hear it. So you'd *better* give him a good reason to have him on speaker tonight." He grabbed her hair and gave her head a violent shake. "Do you understand me?" She nodded. "Okay, here we go."

Cedric tapped Warren's number and then tapped the speaker button before placing the phone near Charli's face.

Charli's thoughts whirled as she waited for him to answer the phone. *Remain calm. Breathe. You can do this.*

He answered.

"Warren! I heard the phone but couldn't get to it. Sorry about that. I was in the kitchen, uh, peeling tomatoes."

A pause and then, "Tomatoes?"

"Yes. And I've got you on speaker because my hands are a mess. I'm, uh, squashing them to make sauce." She glanced at Cedric, who wore a smug expression. "If you want, I can call you back. After I get these tomatoes in the Mason jars."

The silence was longer this time. "Are you all right, Charli?"

"Warren, Warren, Warren. You're so silly. Of course I'm all right. I'm fine." She gave a light chuckle, a sound that in her normal state, she'd never make.

"Did you talk to Griff this evening?"

"Yep, I sure did."

"Is he doing any better?"

"Much. He's already complaining about the cast on his arm. But that bump on the back of his head, the one he got after the cow stepped on him, is starting to go down."

"Wait, you didn't tell me about the cow."

Charli could barely breathe as she watched Cedric's look go from smug to suspicious. He gave a sign for her to wrap it up, then held the gun at her face, point blank.

"Look, Warren, can I call you back? I have to put the tomatoes in the jar while they're hot, otherwise they won't set properly."

"Okay, I'll let you go. But call me back as soon as you're done."

"I'm really exhausted. After I get these tomatoes canned, I'm going directly to bed. See you tomorrow, okay?"

"Sure. Have a good night, sexy. I'm going to miss you."

Cedric ended the call, a sneer on his face. "You did real good, Charli. Handled that like a pro." He leaned down and kissed her on the mouth, then ran his hand over her breasts before kissing her again. "Don't worry. I'm not going to screw you yet. I've been waiting years for this, so I'm going to take my time. After all, your boy won't be expecting to hear from you until morning. We have all night long."

It took all that Charli had not to spit in his face. After he threw up. But there would be time enough to get her revenge, she thought. Her hands were just itching to squeeze a certain set of nuts, just as soon as said hands were untied.

* * *

Warren sat on the edge of his bed, staring at his phone. To say the call was weird would be an understatement. Her voice had sounded okay but she'd called him Warren. Not once, but several times. The only times that happened were either in the throes of passion or at his dogged command. *Something's wrong.* He stood, walked over to the sitting area, replaying the conversation in his head. *I was in the kitchen, uh, peeling tomatoes.* She cooked, so that could very well have been true. "And that would have explained why she was on speakerphone," he mumbled, "and talking more loudly." But what she'd said about Griff. His arm in a cast? Warren could have sworn that it was his leg that had been broken.

He left the master suite and headed down the stairs, still thinking back to the conversation they'd had earlier that day. *His leg is busted up pretty good and he sustained a bruised wrist.* His wrist she'd mentioned, but not his arm. Warren's scowl deepened as he wandered into the living room, and then continued through to the dining room and on to the kitchen.

"She talked to Griff tonight," he murmured, trying to figure out why he felt there was a puzzle to solve, and why the pieces weren't going together. *But wait! Earlier she said he'd had a sleeping pill and would be knocked out till morning.*

He sighed in frustration. *Maybe she was just confused.* They hadn't gotten much sleep the night before and she'd been through a trying day. *Warren, Warren, Warren.* "Maybe she's finally decided to call me by my first name." He laughed. "It's about time."

Feeling a bit more relieved, he walked over to the fridge and after trying to decide what sounded best among his plethora of beverages, he reached for the vegetable juice. He retrieved a glass and watched the red liquid flow. The it hit him. So hard that juice spilled over the counter and the carton ended up in the sink.

When they were in San Francisco. When he'd asked her about breakfast. *Anything but tomatoes. I'm allergic.*

He raced up the stairs and snatched up his cell phone. "Johnny, I need you to come to the house now! I think there's a problem. And bring your weapon."

He ended the call, started to call Charli again, but on second thought quickly tapped another number. Placing the call on speaker, he rushed to his closet to throw on some clothes. Dread replaced the blood running through his veins. "Detective Morrison, this is Warren Drake. I'm calling for an update on Cedric Martin. Have they set his bail yet?"

"They set his bail and it's been posted. He left this afternoon."

"He's free?"

"Yes, he is, Mr. Drake. The charges weren't serious enough to set the bond higher or keep him in—"

Warren hung up the phone, hurried into his shoes and took the stairs two at a time. He opened the front door just as Johnny was about to knock.

"You have your gun on you?"

"Always, Warren. What's going on?"

"Cedric's out," Warren said, rushing to his SUV. "I think he's at Charli's."

"We should call the authorities," Johnny said as he followed.

"We can call them on the way so they can meet us there. But we're not waiting."

They jumped into the car.

"Man, wait!"

"Wait for what?" Warren fired up the engine.

"If he does have her, we have to be smart. We can't

just roll up there and park in the drive. Who knows what he'll do?"

"Okay, we'll park down the street and try to surprise him. But we're going to Charli's place. Now."

Chapter 36

After a quick powwow, Johnny suggested that they use the golf cart, drive across the field and enter her land through the gate by the stream. By coming up the back way, he felt they were more likely to have the element of surprise on their side.

"What about horses? We could leave them by the barn, behind their house. Bobby, her main herd handler, lives not far from there. We might be able to enlist his help as well."

"Sorry, Warren. But the last horse I rode was plastic, went in circles and had a rod through its middle."

Warren gave Johnny a look of exasperation. "The golf cart it is then. Let's go."

While Johnny dialed nine-one-one and then called his second to let him know what was going on, Warren was driving the cart like a racecar, trying to get fifty miles an hour out of a vehicle designed to do twelve. They hit a bump and Johnny went airborne.

He slammed back into the seat. "Slow down, man. Jeez!"

Warren cut him a look and tried to go faster. "Hold on."

Once they'd gone through the gate and were on Reed property, Johnny held out his hand. "Stop for a minute, Warren. This won't work."

Warren reluctantly shut off the engine. "Why?"

"It's too open out here, with too many lights. The white of the cart will reflect off of them. One look out a back window and our goose is cooked."

Warren banged his hands on the wheel, then jumped out of the cart. "We can stay in the shadows as much as we can, crawl if we have to, until we reach those buildings." He pointed in the distance.

"Exactly," Johnny said, as they cautiously started walking. "Then they can shield us. If you have your cell phone on you, make sure it's on Silent."

"Done."

"Man," Johnny whispered as they crept forward, "when I went to the academy, I never thought I'd end up protecting the boy whose older brother used to beat me up in grade school."

"Remind me about that the next time we see Niko. He damn sure owes you now."

Cedric stood, pacing around Charli, who was still tied to the chair. He grasped the bottle of scotch that he'd found on the hutch and drank straight from it.

"I think it's about time that we moved this party into the bedroom," he drawled, taking another swig. "Those wooden slats on your headboard look like they were made for what I have in mind."

Charli tried to keep her torso as still as possible while she continued to work at the knotted rope around her wrist.

"Are you ready to get this party started for real?"

Silence.

He took another drink. "You're not so bad now, are you? Where's that smart mouth now? Where are all those names you called me now?"

"Look, Cedric—"

Smack!

He struck her across the face. Charli immediately tasted blood. She saw red, too. Anger. For his sake, Cedric had better hope that she could not get loose.

"Shut up! In fact—" He slammed down the bottle and grabbed the gun. "I'm tired of messing around with you."

He reached around to where her hands were knotted, the gun to her temple.

And then there was a sound.

Cedric jerked up, looked toward the window where they'd heard it. He looked at Charli, eyes narrowed. "What the hell was that?"

"I don't know!"

There it was again. Sounded like a pebble hitting against the windowpane.

Cedric crept toward the window.

Charli worked on the knot.

"It's probably just the wind," she said, her heartbeat escalating as she felt the knot finally begin to loosen. "One of the shutter panes is loose. It could be knocking against the window."

Cedric looked from her to the window, swaying a bit from the continuous alcohol consumption that had occurred since he'd arrived. He straightened, seeming to have made a decision, and crept toward the door. He placed a hand on the knob, turning it slowly. He opened the door a crack and peeked out.

Go on, get out of here! Charli strained to pull apart the knot.

Cedric opened the door a bit farther.

Then everything happened at once. The knot came loose.

Charli jumped up.

The door crashed in, sending Cedric sprawling backward. He landed at her feet.

That was his bad luck. She picked up the chair he'd tied her to and broke it over his head. After retrieving the gun that had slid across the floor, she was about to aim when Warren crossed the room and caught her arms.

"Charli, no!"

"Let me go, Warren. I'm going to blast that—"

"He's not worth it, baby. Give it to—wait. Is that blood on your mouth? Did he hit you?"

Charli nodded.

Warren let go of her arms. "In that case, blow his balls off."

Cedric tried to draw up his knees against his privates. Warren placed a foot on one of his ankles, preventing that from happening.

Charli aimed. Cocked the trigger. And lowered her arm. "You're right, Drake. He's not worth it."

Still, she walked over to where Johnny had him handcuffed on the ground and kicked him in the groin.

He howled.

Charli leaned down. "Next time I won't just kick them. I will blow them off, just like I promised you I would." She stood. They heard sirens.

"We called the police," Warren said, noting her curious expression. "And if they let him out again, I'll be the one who delivers justice."

Chapter 37

Two days later, Charli walked over to where Warren washed dishes. She placed her arms around his waist and rested her head against his back.

"Breakfast was good, baby," he told her. Silence. He reached for a towel, turning as he dried his hands. He placed a finger under her chin, lifting her eyes up to meet his. "What's wrong?"

"I just got off the phone with my mother."

He hugged her. "How did it go?"

"Better than I expected, actually. She and Pierre are going to come down for Thanksgiving. And she doesn't know it yet, but I'm going to split my portion of the gold with her."

"Good girl."

"Yeah, well, the jury is still out on how good it is."

"Like Miss Alice said, it's the right thing to do, babe."

The conversation was interrupted by the sound of a car coming up the driveway. "I wonder who that could be,"

Charli said as she walked toward the door. "Miss Alice?" She opened the screen. *And Griff?*

"What in the heck is going on here?" she asked, coming off the porch and toward Miss Alice's car. She reached the passenger side. "Griff, what are you doing here?"

He gave her a look. "It's where I live."

"You know what I mean," she said, swatting his arm, wanting to hug him and hit him at the same time. "What are you doing out of the hospital? Miss Alice, what's going on?"

"Griff being Griff is what's going on. The doctors told him they wanted to keep him for a few more days and Griff told them he was leaving." She opened the trunk and pulled out a portable wheelchair. "Here, Charli, help me with this thing."

Warren, who'd stepped out on the porch, now came down. "I've got it, Miss Alice. Griff, how are you doing?"

"Fair to middlin'."

"You'll probably be better after a shot, huh?"

"That's exactly right."

Charli, who'd knelt down to hug the old man, had tears in her eyes. "You should have called me. I would have come to get you."

Griff looked past her at Warren, then back at her. "Looks like you had your hands just about full."

Between the crutches, the wheelchair and Warren's strength, they got Griff into the house and settled in his recliner. His favorite bottle of homemade liquor, a shot glass and his pouch of tobacco were all within reach.

At first there was small talk: about his hospital stay, the state of the cattle and Warren's finished house. But after taking a drink and filling his jaw, Griff settled back into the chair. "Now stop dillydallying and tell me about the mess we've got going on round here."

One by one, they did. "Cedric was charged with break

ing and entering, assault with a deadly weapon, unlawful restraint and a few other things that I can't remember," Warren finished. "He's going to have a while to think about what he did."

"What about the others? Do you know who they are?"

"No," Charli responded.

"Well, actually, babe, there's been a development. They found a lone fingerprint on the door to the secure room where the gold is kept. A warrant has been issued for his arrest."

"Who is it?" Charli asked.

"Richard."

"The friend you hired?"

Warren snorted. "Obviously not such a friend, since he tried to steal from me. And to think my mom was kind enough to want to give him a chance, and I was dumb enough to go along."

"You were showing that you have a heart, Drake, ready to give the man a second chance."

"Yes, and he reverted right back to his criminal ways. He was living in paradise, a great place to make a new start. And he blew it."

"Are they sure it was him? It's so hard to think someone would steal from the very man who signed his paychecks."

"It was him. Even before they found the print, I thought it was mighty convenient that he left town right after the break-in happened. Mighty suspect, too." He looked at his watch. "Charli, we need to go. I told Mom I'd meet her at the house."

"I'm sorry, Drake. But I can't leave. Not with Griff here."

"Now, honey, you just go on," Miss Alice said, getting to fluff the pillow beneath Griff's leg. "Me and Griff will be just fine, here. Won't we, Griff?"

Neither Warren nor Charli missed the quick, affectionate pat she gave him.

"Okay, guys. But I'll be back tonight, in time to cook supper."

Again, Miss Alice spoke up. "Don't worry about that, either. Me and Griff have already talked about it and I'm going to stay here for a spell, while he's on the mend. I've got my suitcases in the car. I'll get them later. So don't you worry about a thing. Just go on and take care of your man."

Suitcases, as in plural? Charli suddenly realized it might not have been her grandfather that Miss Alice was digging back in the day…but someone else.

"Well, I'll see you both later on tonight, then. I won't be out too late. And I'll be sure and call and tell you that I'm on my way."

Minutes later, Warren and Charli were in his SUV, laughing about the turn of events with Griff and Miss Alice.

"That's pitiful," Charli said with a shake of her head. "I don't see how they think he's going to get his groove on sitting up there with a broken leg."

"Baby," Warren said, reaching over and taking her hand. "Not all of his legs are broken."

Chapter 38

"Wasn't this a great idea, darling? I told you that we should go ahead with the party."

"Yes, Mom."

Warren hugged his mother as they stood just inside the living room entrance. The room was filled with some of Paradise Cove's elite, mingling with gold miners and farmhands. A great idea indeed.

Looking at his watch, he removed his arm from around his mother's shoulders. "I think I'm going to call Charli again. They should have been here by now."

"Now, Warren. Don't be anxious. Every woman worth her salt likes to make a late entrance."

"With Griff at home recuperating, I'm afraid there won't be an entrance at all!"

They laughed and watched as one of the guests walked over to join them. "Jennifer Drake! You look lovely."

They exchanged air kisses.

"Alice, it's been too long."

"Not so long ago, sweetie. Just since the Days of Paradise Ball."

"Of course."

"Warren, you look good." Alice's eyes swept over him appreciatively. "My niece had better hurry up and get here, snatch you up before I give her some competition!"

Jennifer chuckled. "Alice, have you tried the caviar? It was flown in from Italy."

"Girl, the only eggs I eat come from a hen."

"Well, I'm sure there's something on the buffet that you'll enjoy. Oh, and there's Bonnie. Let's go and say hello."

Niko came over, his eyes twinkling. "What was that about?"

"Mom being her usual self—trying to control every thing."

"Speaking of controlling things, looks like we both dodged a bullet."

"How do you figure?"

"Long story that I'll fill you in on later, but the short of it is…I'm no longer seeing Ashley."

"I know Mom is happy."

"Thrilled. And she was right, too, about Ashley's ulterior motives. I just hope that Ash understands that it's over between us."

"It may take a while, but I think she'll move on." Warren thought about the recent conversation he'd had with Rachel, when he'd told her about his relationship with Charli. Though they'd never dated and Warren had never led her on, he and Rachel had known each other since childhood. He sincerely wished her every happiness.

"The town is too small for them not to know about the party. But so far, neither Rachel nor Ashley has decided to crash it."

"Brother, please. I've had enough unwanted guests on my property to last me a lifetime!"

Both men laughed, then turned as they heard the tinkling bells, signaling that the outer door was being opened. "Excuse me, brother." Warren walked down the foyer. "Dad. Grandpa." He gave each man a hug.

"This place is great, son," Ike said, looking around. "Jackson did himself proud."

"That he did."

The men bypassed the crowded living room, went down the hall and into one of Warren's favorite places: his home office and library, fashioned after his dad's. They also toured the theater, solarium and six-car garage.

"Let's go out this way," Warren said, walking toward the garage door. "So I can show you a little extra something that Jackson installed."

He opened the side door to the garage, stepped out and saw something totally unexpected: Charli walking up the drive...pushing Griff in a wheelchair. Directly behind him came his grandfather and dad.

Oh, boy.

Without looking back, he walked over. "Babe! You look gorgeous!" He gave her a hug and quick kiss on the lips. "You don't look bad, either," he said to Griff.

But Griff wasn't listening. He was looking beyond Warren to the man who was staring back at him. Warren straightened and turned around. "Grandpa, come on over here."

Later, he would find out that Ike had had to prod him, but Walter Drake was soon at Warren's side.

"You remember Griff, don't you, Grandpa?"

"Unfortunately."

"Griff, you remember my grandfather, Walter?"

"I'da had to fall off a taller ladder to forget."

Walter took a step forward. "I am surprised to see you though. I thought you'd died."

"If I'd known the choice was death or seeing your ugly mug again, I might have chosen glory."

Charli stepped between them. "All right, you two. Enough." She stood squarely before Walter and held out he hand. "I'm Charli Reed, your former best friend's grand daughter. Your grandson Warren thinks a great deal c you and since I know that he's a good judge of characte it is my pleasure to meet you."

Griff snorted. Charli cut him a look.

At the same time, Warren gave Walter a warning glanc

Walter stuck out his hand. "You're Cherise's girl?"

"You know my mother?"

"Of course, though the last time I saw her she was sti quite young. Pretty little girl, as I remember. The app didn't fall far from the tree."

"Thank you, Mr. Drake. I appreciate the complimer But honestly, what I'd like even more is for you and Gri to bury the hatchet of hatred between you. You two haver seen each other in years and my grandfather is dead. Wha ever happened back then can't be undone. But what ha pens from this moment forward can be a new chapter our lives."

She stepped back, no longer the barrier between Walt and Griff. The two men warily eyed each other. Soun from some of the guests obviously enjoying the patio ar drifted toward them. A howl sounded in the distance, fe lowed by a chorus of barking dogs.

"Well, Dad," Ike finally said. "We're waiting."

Walter took one step. And then another. "I can let k gones be bygones, Griff. What about you?"

Griff looked from Walter to Ike to Warren and th back to Walter. "Fine young man right there," he said w a nod in Warren's direction. "Fair and decent." He look at Warren. "I read over the contract you sent, the one concerning the gold on both our lands. I'll admit that it surprised me, the terms, that is."

Looking between Ike and Walter, he continued, "Got my dander up at first, when I saw where he paid all the expenses for the dig. We've never been ones to accept charity, or have our hand out." Finally, his eyes rested on Charli. "Then I thought about you, and how he's never treated you in any way less than a lady. That's when I had to admit the truth, that you're a Drake. And you're a good man."

He lifted his hand toward Walter. "Guess that means the ones who raised him have some good in them, too."

Walter smiled, nodding as he shook Griff's hand.

"Whew, finally," Warren said.

Charli blinked back tears as she gave Walter a hug. "Thank you," she whispered. "I never thought I'd see this day."

Warren stepped behind the wheelchair, ready to help Griff inside. "Let's go inside, y'all. This calls for a toast."

"Wait! We don't have to go nowhere for that." Griff reached between his hip and the chair. "I've got the toast right here." He pulled out a silver flask.

Walter looked at Griff, his expression dubious. "Don't tell me you're still making that hooch."

"All right," Griff said, handing him the flask. "I won't."

Walter unscrewed the top on the flask and took a sniff. "Whew! A sniff alone would cure the common cold."

"Come on, Grandpa," Warren teased. "Don't be a lightweight."

"Boy, what do you know about it?"

Warren made to grab the flask, but Walter moved it out of his reach. "Wait now. Let a man show you how it's done." He took a healthy swig, swallowed and immediately began coughing.

"You all right, Grandpa?" Warren asked, slapping the old man on the back.

"I forgot how strong Griff made this stuff. Man, that will put hair on your chest!"

Warren and Griff said nothing, just looked at each other and smiled.

They went inside, the night wore on and everyone agreed on two things: Warren's home was spectacular and the party was a great success. At the height of it, Warren reached for a flute of champagne, hitting a fork against the crystal until the tinkling sound got everyone's attention and one by one they quieted down.

"I just wanted to take a moment and thank all of you for coming. And I wanted to thank my party planner extraordinaire mother for helping me put this on."

Jennifer gave a little bow and blew a kiss to her son.

"I also want to recognize my grandfather, who has been in town for a short while, Walter Drake, and my grandmother, who flew in this morning to join us."

Walter and Claire, who were now standing next to each other, gave small waves.

Warren acknowledged his father and the rest of his family. "And finally," he said once they'd waved their greetings, "I want to thank someone else. Charli," he said, looking across the room at where she stood next to Miss Alice and Griff. "Could you come here, please?"

At first Charli shrank back with a quick shake of her head. Public speaking wasn't her thing. Unless the audience was cows.

"Go on, girl," Miss Alice whispered, giving her a little push.

Charli's brow creased at this unexpected invitation before she slowly walked over to where Warren stood. She stopped next to him and looked up.

"Charli Reed is my neighbor, owner of the Reed Ranch

ler family and mine have a history that dates back gen-
rations, when her grandfather, Charles, and my grandfa-
ner—" he nodded at Walter "—were partners. Mr. Griff
ohnson—" Warren raised his glass to Griff, seated in the
heelchair "—was also a significant part of their opera-
on, and continues to help run their dairy business.

"I tell you all this because when I first moved here, they
ere strangers. Then they became my neighbors and now
ley are like family. Well, almost."

He turned to Charli. "Charli, from the time you rode up
that horse like you owned the world, I was captivated."

Charli took a deep breath. Her heart began to pound.

"You were demanding, rude—" a few people giggled,
ne of them Griff "—irreverent, opinionated, and all I
anted was to be around you. My love."

He pulled out a box. She gasped softly as her hands
ent to her mouth. "I want to be around you for the rest
my life."

He went down on one knee. "Charlene…Charli Reed…
ll you marry me?"

She nodded, slowly at first and then more vigorously
d then, realizing that she should probably say it out loud,
sponded, "Yes!"

There were cheers and applause and oohs and ahhs as
women gathered around to see the ring. It was not your
erage engagement ring. There were no diamonds, noth-
; jutting up to get snagged in the hay or dig into Charli's
d when she was roping. Just an intricately designed
d made of solid gold.

"Do you like it?" he asked moments later when they
ped outside for a few stolen moments alone.

'It's perfect," she whispered. "Exactly what I would
e chosen."

'Just so you know," he said, turning her toward him

and wrapping his arms around her. "This marks the end of my seduction."

"Oh, is that what you've been doing all these months?"

He nodded.

"Well, yours might be over," she said, running her hand precariously close to his treasures. "But mine has only just begun."

* * * * *

REQUEST YOUR FREE BOOKS!

2 FREE NOVELS
PLUS 2 *FREE GIFTS!*

KIMANI™
ROMANCE

Love's ultimate destination!

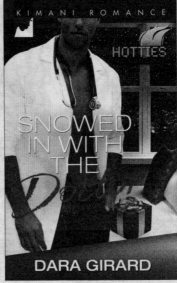